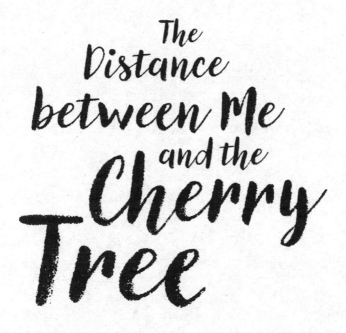

The
Distance
between Me
and the
Cherry
Tree

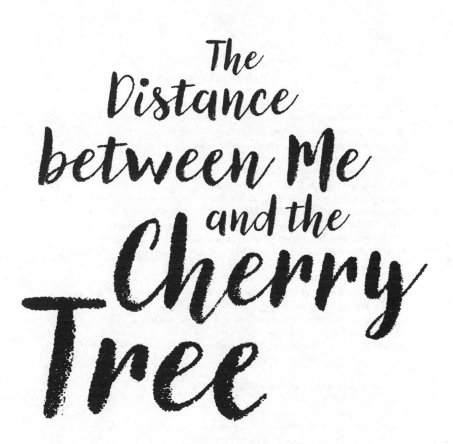

The Distance between Me and the Cherry Tree

PAOLA PERETTI

Translated by Denise Muir

Illustrated by Carolina Rabei

Atheneum Books for Young Readers
New York London Toronto Sydney New Delhi

ATHENEUM BOOKS FOR YOUNG READERS

An imprint of Simon & Schuster Children's Publishing Division
1230 Avenue of the Americas, New York, New York 10020

ATHENEUM BOOKS FOR YOUNG READERS is a registered trademark of Simon & Schuster, Inc. Atheneum logo is a trademark of Simon & Schuster, Inc.
For information about special discounts for bulk purchases, please contact Simon & Schuster Special Sales at 1-866-506-1949 or business@simonandschuster.com.
The Simon & Schuster Speakers Bureau can bring authors to your live event. For more information or to book an event, contact the Simon & Schuster Speakers Bureau at 1-866-248-3049 or visit our website at www.simonspeakers.com.
Jacket design by Debra Sfetsios-Conover; interior design by Tom Daly
The text for this book was set in AdobeCaslon Pro.
The illustrations for this book were rendered digitally.
Manufactured in the United States of America
0819 FFG
First Atheneum Books for Young Readers edition September 2019
10 9 8 7 6 5 4 3 2 1
Library of Congress Cataloging-in-Publication Data
Names: Peretti, Paola, author. | Muir, Denise, translator. | Rabei, Carolina, illustrator.
Title: The distance between me and the cherry tree / Paola Peretti ; translated by Denise Muir ; illustrated by Carolina Rabei.
Other titles: La distanza tra me e il ciliegio. English
Description: First edition. | New York : Atheneum, [2019] |
Summary: When nine-year-old Mafalda learns she will go blind in six months from Stargardt Disease, she needs the help of family and friends to retain what is essential to her.
Identifiers: LCCN 2018057766 | ISBN 9781534439627 (hardcover) | ISBN 9781534439641 (eBook)
Subjects: | CYAC: Blind—Fiction. | People with disabilities—Fiction. | Family life—Fiction. | Friendship—Fiction.
Classification: LCC PZ7.1.P44745 Dis 2019 | DDC [Fic]—dc23
LC record available at https://lccn.loc.gov/2018057766

Part One

Seventy Meters

The Dark

All children are scared of the dark.

The dark is a room with no door and no windows, where monsters grab you and eat you without making a sound.

I'm not afraid of the dark, though.

But I have something else to worry about. I have my very own dark, the one in my eyes.

I'm not making it up. If I were, Mom wouldn't buy me pastries shaped like peaches filled with cream and she wouldn't let me eat them before dinner. If everything were okay, Dad wouldn't hide in the bathroom when the landlady phones, because it's always bad news when she calls.

"Don't worry," Mom says when she does the dishes after dinner. "Go and play in your room and don't worry about a thing."

I hesitate in the kitchen doorway, trying with the power of my mind to make her turn round, but it never works. So here I am in my room, cuddling Ottimo Turcaret, my brown-and-gray cat with a kink at the end of his tail. He doesn't mind being lifted, rolled over on the carpet, or chased with the toilet brush. He's a cat, Dad says, and cats are opportunists. I suppose that means they like attention. For me, it's enough that he's around when things are going wrong and I need something warm and cuddly to hug. Like now.

I know something's wrong. I might only be in fifth grade, but I notice everything. My cousin's girlfriend says I have a third eye. She's Indian, and I like that she thinks I have an extra eye, although it would be better if the two eyes I already have actually worked.

Sometimes I feel like crying, like now. My glasses steam up when I'm about to cry. I take them off, so at least they can dry and the red mark on my nose will go away. I've worn glasses since I started elementary school. I got these yellow ones with sparkly bits in

December last year, and I love them. I put them back on in front of the mirror. Without my glasses, everything's a bit misty, like when I have a very hot shower with boiling hot water. My mist is called Stargardt mist, or so Mom and Dad told me. They must've heard about it at the hospital. It says on Dad's phone that Mr. Stargardt was a German ophthalmologist who lived a hundred years ago; he worked out what's going on with my eyes. He also discovered that people who have the same mist as me see black spots in front of things or people, and that these spots get bigger and bigger, until they're huge, and people with the spots have to get closer to things to see them properly. The Internet says, "The disease affects one in ten thousand people." Mom says that special people are chosen by God, but when I think about it, I don't feel that lucky.

Things I Care a Lot About (That I Won't Be Able to Do Anymore)

Today I can see myself in the mirror from three steps away.

This distance is getting shorter. A year ago, I could see myself from five steps.

I pet Ottimo Turcaret's head in front of the mirror and, while I'm here, smooth my own hair. Mom likes putting pigtails in my hair these days and doesn't like me messing them up. She likes them so much, she even has me keep them in at night.

Dad pops his head round the door and tells me to "pajamify" and brush my teeth. I say okay but stand at the window for ages before I do what he asks. You can see a huge patch of dark sky from the window in my bedroom. I like leaning out on autumn nights like these; it's not cold and you can see the moon and the North Star shining bright. Mom says they're Jesus's streetlamp and match. I'm more interested in checking that they're both still there every night.

Dad comes in to read a story before I go to sleep. We're halfway through *Robin Hood* at the moment, and it's filling my dreams with forests and bows and arrows. Mom usually comes in after to arrange my pigtails on my pillow; she lays them out around my face and says good night, mint on her breath.

They come in together tonight and sit on either side of my bed. They say they've noticed I'm seeing a little less and have decided to take me to a specialist next week. I don't like skipping school because I miss important information (like how long it took to build the pyramids) and gossip (Are Chiara and Gianluca really dating?). But I don't say this to Mom and Dad. I wait for them to leave the room and turn the big light off, and then I turn on my bedside lamp. I run my fingers over the edge of the books behind my head, on the shelf above the headboard. I pick up the notebook with the crumpled corner.

I lay it on my pillow. The label on the front of it says: MAFALDA'S LIST.

I use this notebook as my personal organizer. There's a date—September 14—on the first page. That was three years, eleven days ago. Under that, I've written:

> *Things I care a lot about*
> *(that I won't be able to do anymore)*

It's not a long list. There are only three pages, to tell the truth, and the first one starts with:

> *Counting the stars in the sky at night*
> *Driving a submarine*
> *Making good-night light signals at the*
> *window*

Code red. My glasses have steamed up.

Grandma used to live across the road from us, in the red house with lace curtains. A young couple lives there now. They never say hello and have even changed the curtains. Grandma was Dad's mom. She had hair like mine, only gray, and would always wave her flashlight to me before going to bed. One flash meant, "I'm calling you." Two flashes, "Good night." Three flashes, "You too." But that was before, when I could still see myself in the mirror from nine steps.

I never show the second page to anyone, not even to Ottimo Turcaret, because it's extremely top secret, so secret I only ever write in code.

The third page says:

> *Playing soccer*
> *Playing my pavement game where if you fall off*
>   *the lines, you end up in the lava and die*
> *Having a paper-ball-in-the-basket competition*
> *Climbing up the school cherry tree*

I've climbed the school cherry tree loads of times, since my first day at elementary school. It's my tree. None of the other children can climb as high as I can. When I was little, I would stroke the trunk, hug it—it was my friend. In fact, I found Ottimo Turcaret in the tree. He was terrified, and the same brown and gray as he is now, only uglier. He was so tiny, I brought him home in my pocket, and it was only when I pulled him out and sat him on the table that Mom and Dad realized he was a real kitten.

He wasn't called Ottimo Turcaret then. He didn't

have a name, but after he'd been with us a while and followed me everywhere, even to school, Dad gave me his favorite book, *The Baron in the Trees*, as a present and read it to me at bedtime. That's where I met Cosimo. He's a boy, a bit older than me—not much, though—and he lived a long time ago when people wore wigs and tried to force him to do boring homework and eat disgusting food. He had a dachshund with two names, and we decided that Ottimo Turcaret definitely looked like an Ottimo Turcaret, even though our cat doesn't have two owners like the dachshund, which was called Ottimo Massimo when it was with Cosimo, and Turcaret when it was with Viola, its real owner.

My favorite person in the book is Cosimo—I love that he goes to live in the trees and never comes back down because he wants to be free. I'd be too scared. I tried to build a tree house in the cherry tree with toilet paper once, but it rained and the walls dissolved. The thing I liked best, though, was to take a comic book up and read it on a branch that had split in two. I could still see quite well then.

Every year since I started school, I've had an eye exam with drops that burn. The doctors call it a "routine test." I think the specialist tests next week might be a bit different because my pilot light, the one in my eyes, seems to be in a hurry to go out. A very big hurry. The ophthalmologist explained it to me. She's not German like Mr. Stargardt and hasn't discovered anything, but she always gives me a pencil with a colorful eraser at the end. She told me the light goes out in some people when they're old, a bit earlier in others. Mine will go out completely while I'm still young.

I'll be left in the dark, she said.

I don't want to think about it just now. All I want to do is dream about forests and Robin Hood shooting arrows.

I shut my notebook and switch off the light.

Cosimo, can you help me?

You can do anything you set your mind to, and you're kind. I know you are because in the book, you read stories to the brigand even though he'd been very bad. You read them through the prison bars until the day he was hanged, didn't you? What about me? Who'll read to me? Who'll read me stories when I'm left in the dark and Mom and Dad are at work?

If even you, a friend of the trees like me, can't help, I might stop speaking to you. Worse still, I'll stop thinking about you. Please find a way to help me, even secretly. You don't have to tell me—just find one, or I'll make the branches under your bottom disappear with my mind and you'll fall into the lava with the crocodiles, or to the ground, which is worse seeing as you swore never to come down from the trees.

Estella always says we can get by on our own, that we don't need anything. Well, I need a really big something. Will you promise, Cosimo? Will you help me?

The Amazon Game

Estella gave me the idea for the list the day we met three years and eleven days ago, when she came from Romania to be at my school.

I was in the playground, up in the cherry tree. The bell had rung and I was stuck.

"You stuck, no?"

I looked down from the tree, eyes screwed up, and pushed aside a branch with lots of yellow leaves on it. Standing near the tree, arms crossed, was a janitor I'd never seen at school before. She was tall and had dark hair, and even though I couldn't see what color her eyes were, they looked really big and really black and almost scared me.

"Well, I help. Then you go school."

I sat motionless in the tree, frightened I might fall.

"Put foot here." The janitor with the scary eyes was pointing to a piece of trunk jutting out just below me. I was holding on tight to the branch I was sitting on. I tried to lower my foot, but it slipped, and the bark cracked under my weight. I went straight back to my original position.

"I'm not coming down."

"You stay up rest of life?"

"Yes."

"Bye, then." The janitor took a step toward the school. There was a crunching sound under her feet. She bent down and picked up a pair of red glasses. They'd been hidden in the leaves.

"What's this? Is yours?"

"They're my glasses. They fell when I was climbing up. And now I can't get back down!"

"No cry. Not need." The lady with the black in her eyes was back below my branch. "You know, in Romania I always climb trees. I liked play at top."

I sniffed and asked what games she played.

"I made the game . . . what you call it . . . Amazon. You know what is Amazon?"

"No, what is it?"

"Amazon is female warrior on horse. Not afraid to come down tree."

"But she doesn't wear glasses."

"No. She very strong. Afraid of nothing. She cut off piece of breast to fire bow and arrow."

"A piece of her breast?"

"Yes. The grandmother of the grandmother of my grandmother was from an Amazon family, long time ago."

"That's not true."

"It is."

The lady with the scary black eyes was hurriedly rolling up her shirtsleeves. Then she started climbing up the tree. I clung to my branch. When she reached me, she sat down beside me like she was riding a horse.

"See? Amazon."

"But how will we get down now?"

She took my glasses out of her shirt pocket and handed them to me. I put them on right away. They were a bit dusty and crooked, but at least I could see better.

"You follow me now," the janitor said. Up close, I could see she also had very bright pink lipstick. She started to descend as quickly as she'd climbed up.

"Wait!"

"What?"

"I don't want to come down."

"Good the God! Come down—I must work!"

I felt bad about wasting her time. She had been nice bringing up my glasses, but I didn't want to come down because the day before, Doctor Olga had said I had a bad thing in my eyes and I was frightened.

I felt better in the tree. Nothing could happen to me here.

I told the lady this. I also explained that I couldn't see very well and it was going to get worse. I said that I didn't want to not be able to climb the tree anymore.

"If there are things you can't do anymore, you must write list. That way you not forget anything."

"A list?"

"Of course. List. I make list too, years ago."

"Could you not see well either?"

"No. It wasn't that."

"What was wrong, then?"

The lady sighed and set off back down the tree.

"I had less problem than now, you pain in neck."

I followed her gingerly, edging along my branch. I was a bit miffed at what she'd said, but I was also curious.

"What was on your list?"

"Come down, I show you. What's your name?"

"Mafalda. And yours?"

"Estella."

Estella jumped down from the bottom branch of the cherry tree and turned to face me.

I'd reached the lower branches and had also jumped. She caught me in midair and placed me firmly on the ground. Then she walked over to the main entrance of the school, but not before she held out her hand and called my name. "Mafalda. Estella does not tell lies. Only truth. We go see Estella's list."

I see Estella now every day at school.

When I get there at ten minutes to eight, she's at the door waiting for me. She makes our secret signal—a whistle loud enough to burst your eardrums—which everyone hears, though, so it's not really that secret. She does it with two fingers in her mouth. I don't know anyone else who can whistle like that. I hear it from far, far away, and I run to meet her.

But first, I stop to greet the cherry tree. I can see it from a long way away (well, quite far away) on the road I take every morning with Dad. In truth, all I actually see is a colored blob in front of me, but I know it's the tree—I mean, the giant's hair, if the giant is as nice as I imagine him.

Grandma always said that there are giants living

inside the trunks of trees, giant tree spirits that move away to another tree when theirs gets chopped down. There used to be a cherry tree in Grandma's garden. I climbed it all the time when I was small. I'd help Grandma pick the ripened cherries. I didn't even need glasses.

Right away, we'd make a cake with the cherries, or maybe jam to eat in winter. Grandma's tree got infected with a sort of tree lice, though, and we had to cut it down. I thought cutting the leaves off would have been enough. When we get head lice at school, they don't kill us, do they? They just wash our hair with smelly shampoo.

When they chopped it down, I decided that the giant had gone to live in the cherry tree at school and that he'd taken Grandma's spirit with him, and that it would be fun to count how many steps there are between the tree and when I can see it. That way I'd know how close I am to Grandma's giant. I screw my eyes up and try my best and, finally, yes, there it is—a red, yellow, and orange blob, like the wigs clowns wear. It's all blurry, but it's there. The school next to it is a blue blob. I start counting right away: one, two, three. . . .

"Come on, Mafalda, we'll be late if you walk like that," Dad says, gently tugging my hand.

"Dad, how long is one of my steps?"

"Hmm, I'm not sure. It must be about fifty centimeters. You're quite tall for your age."

I keep counting. I count thirty steps before I hear Estella whistle. Thirty-five, thirty-six . . . forty, fifty, one hundred. We reach the school gates. Estella comes to meet me, says hello to Dad. I pick up a leaf near the tree. It's wet and yellow on the front, brown on the back. It is perfectly shaped and smells earthy. It reminds me of working in the garden with Grandma. I slip it into my pocket as Estella takes me inside.

It took me one hundred and forty steps to reach the cherry tree from where I started to see it.

Seventy meters.

Part Two

Sixty Meters

4

The Bit in the Middle of the Eye

The second page of my list is the most important, to me anyway, and because it's supersecret, I put it between two pages. That way, if anyone steals my personal organizer and reads the first page, they'll think there's nothing special in it.

To tell the truth, the first and third pages are important too; it's just that the second one is the most important. I've written things on it that I would never tell anyone. I write them in my special code, just like Sherlock Holmes did for his secret things. I'm going to see Doctor Olga in a bit and am waiting for Mom to finish putting her makeup on while I pretend to cuddle Ottimo Turcaret on the balcony. What I'm really doing is peeking at the second page of my list. Estella said I shouldn't do this because once I've written these things down, I should let them go or keep them to myself. I don't really understand what this means, so I've decided that I'll read the second page when I feel up to it. Until it's a bit clearer what she means.

I hear Mom's heels approaching. She always wears heels when we go to the doctor. I snap my personal organizer shut and hide it under the chair.

"Are you ready? Let's go."

I'll think about it later, that thing Estella said. She says so many things that I'll be in the dark before I understand what any of them mean.

Doctor Olga has green eyes, I think.

She sits at her desk and gives me a pencil with a dinosaur eraser on the end.

"Don't you have one with Egyptian gods?" I ask. Mom, sitting beside me, elbows me. Dad is here too, with a smart jacket over his coveralls. He's on his lunch hour, but today he has to be with us at the hospital because the results of my tests have arrived. The doctor says she'll get some pencils with Egyptian gods, in case other children ask for them. Then she gets serious.

"I'm sorry to say that things are not great. Mafalda's retina has thinned very quickly over the past few months. The tissue won't be able to hold out much longer. The macula—"

"That's the bit in the middle of my eye," I interject, to help Mom and Dad understand. "We studied it at school."

"The very one. Mafalda's macula has been severely compromised, as the test results show."

I'm not sure I understand what she's saying, although it occurs to me that maybe I could have tried harder in the tests. I didn't stand completely still when they put the wires in my eyes, and I even nodded off during the red dot test! I'm about to say this to the doctor, but she keeps speaking, in tones so hushed I have to point my ear to her mouth to hear.

"The speed with which the disease has advanced doesn't leave us much hope. Optimistically . . ."

"How long?" Dad asks, his voice even quieter, something that never happens.

"Optimistically . . . six months."

Mom and Dad crumple in their seats like burst balloons. I, on the other hand, lean toward the desk and ask the doctor, "Six months before what?"

She looks at me through glasses with thin lenses. "Before you can't see anymore, Mafalda."

"So, I'm really going to end up in the dark?"

She hesitates. "I'm sorry" is all she says.

My glasses steam up.

Some kinds of news should only be given if you have a cat on hand to hug.

5

Having a Best Friend

When we get home from the doctor's, I pick up Ottimo Turcaret and use him as a blanket for my dream nap.

I had my first dream nap last year, when my cousin Andrea started going out with Ravina. Ravina taught me something called meditation, which means a way to have lovely dreams even if you're sad or angry or not very sleepy. You have to be as quiet as a mouse and imagine you're inside your body, which is not that nice at first, but you get used to it and after a bit you stop thinking about the blood pulsing in your veins and to your brain, and you find yourself thinking about nothing at all. Well, that's what happens to me. Noises around the house caress my face in waves, like bells chiming in the distance, and I end up falling asleep. That's when the dreams come.

Today's nap brings a lovely dream.

I dream that I climb up the cherry tree at school, to the highest branch, up, up, at the top. I can see the whole town—no, the whole world—from up here. I open my arms and start to fly. I fly up to the roof of the school, then higher still. In the end I fly away. To the moon and the North Star, although I can see all the stars clearly too. I play soccer with Grandma, who is in the goal.

Chiara comes around to play, but not soccer. Mom called her, although I'd rather be by myself. I'm learning to read with braille dots, and the book Estella gave me to practice with is really good and also a bit strange. It's called *The Little Prince*, and she bought it online. Chiara's my friend from nursery school, and I can't just pretend she's not here. To be honest, she hasn't been over to play at my house, or invited me to hers, for ages. The last time was her birthday in June, and we both went away on vacation after that.

I put the dot alphabet away when she arrives. She sees it all the same and immediately asks me what

I'm doing. "Nothing," I reply. I don't know why, but I'd rather she didn't see me reading with braille dots. I feel stupid. I suggest we go into my bedroom to play restaurants because I know she likes to cook and always watches *MasterChef*.

We set a table with plastic plates and cutlery. I can no longer find the fake glasses, so we fill up two real glasses with water. Chiara plays the waiter and chef; I'm the customer. I pretend to look at the menu and pick all the complicated dishes. Chiara has fun writing them on her hand and repeating them (incorrectly) to the chef in the kitchen, which is my open wardrobe, and then she pretends to start cooking.

The restaurant game's okay, though I'm not crazy about it, so after we've done the same scene three times, I suggest we play husband-and-wife-who-go-out-for-dinner, to mix it up a bit. We say goodbye to Ottimo Turcaret, who's staying at home with the babysitter— that's my doll Maggie—and sit down at our table. Right away we both have the same idea (it's like that with best friends) to experiment with the ingredients in our drinks. We run around the house looking for disgusting things to put in them: earth from the plant pots, salt and pepper, a spray of Dad's aftershave, even a bit of dried glue stick that looks like snail slime. We mix them together with a fork and go back to our table.

"I propose a toast," Chiara says. She raises her glass full of yellowy gunk and pretends to drink. I reach out a hand to pick up mine—it's right there on my left, I think. But my eye goes dark and instead of picking it up, my fingers bump the glass and knock it over onto Chiara, who starts screaming because the disgusting gunk is all over her leggings. The dark fills with glimmering spiders. I can't see a thing; I only hear the glass roll away, then the sound of it breaking by my feet. Mom rushes in wanting to know what's happened.

Chiara demands to go home even though it's not four o'clock yet. I hear her mom, who came in for a coffee, speak to her in the hallway. The black blob in my left eye is gradually fading, but Chiara and her mom are already by the front door, car keys in hand.

"See you at school," I say, sticking my head out into the hallway. Chiara just replies with a short "bye" and leaves. Mom shuts the door and walks over to me, a wet cloth in her hand. "Do you want a sandwich with chocolate spread?"

Grandma would have made it with jam.

I go back into my room and pick up *The Little Prince* again. I pretend to read. Mom goes slowly back into the kitchen, and I pull out my personal organizer. I open it at the second page, the supersecret one, and with a black pen cross out the words, *Having a best friend.*

6

He Wears Them Too

I like the Little Prince, but my *most favorite* character of all is Cosimo. It's Dad's favorite book because Grandma gave it to him as a present when he was in secondary school. She said she knew the author, that they were friends, that she even sort of *loved* him. I don't really understand this. The way I see it, you either like a person and you are friends, or you love them. They are two different things and can't be *sort of* the same thing. Grandma used to say that friends are for reading books with, like Cosimo and the brigand, so I'm sure Cosimo and I could have read lots of books together, if we'd met.

Today is All Saints' Day, a public holiday here in Italy, so there's no school.

I go with Mom and Dad to the graveyard to visit Grandma and other dead relatives I have never met.

I used to like the graveyard because it's paved with black and white stones, like a chessboard, and I liked jumping on them. Last year, though, I tripped a lady by mistake and was told to stop. Now I get really bored at the graveyard. Grandma's headstone is ugly—it has an angel with a silly face on it. Grandma didn't believe in angels, although she always said I was her angel.

A group of children are playing soccer in the square outside the graveyard today. A few are in my class. There's also an older boy who is always causing trouble and getting into fights at school. I know it's him by the blue jacket with his name written across the back. Filippo. He's the only one with a jacket like that. Who knows where he got it.

Chiara is there too, sitting on a wall in the parking garage. I ask Mom if I can hang out with them while she and Dad finish their tour of the dead relatives.

"Okay, but don't wander off."

Mom says this all the time. Where does she think I'd go?

I go over to Chiara, who's chatting with another

girl from our grade. They say hello but go straight back to their conversation. It doesn't matter; I'm more interested in playing soccer. I trained for a year with a mixed team in third grade. I was goalie. I stopped when a ball broke my glasses, but I'd still like to play in secret.

The boys are picking teams. I can't see how many of them there are because it's a bit hazy from a distance, but I can hear Marco, one of my classmates, saying he has to go. His parents have finished at the graveyard. I can always hear all the words, no matter how far away I am, and all the sounds. When an ambulance is coming, I hear it before everyone else—at school, at home, everywhere I go. Doctor Olga says my hearing has become more developed because my sight is so poor. This doesn't make me feel lucky, though.

If Marco goes home, I should be able to play. I go over to the group and ask if I can take his place.

Filippo peers over his glasses at me. He wears them too, although they are less noticeable because they're clear.

"No chance. You're a girl. You don't know how to play."

"That's not true. I played goalie for a year. Ask him."

I point to another boy in my class, Kevin. The others turn to look at him.

"Yes, she did; she was on my team. But I'm not sure if . . ."

I think he's afraid I might mess up and let a goal in.

"I can dive, too," I tell Filippo. "Put me in the goal."

He gives me a doubtful look. The others say nothing, except for one boy who complains that I'm a girl.

"If you don't want to play, go home," Filippo says, pushing him away. The boy who complained is angry but decides to hang around. While they're deciding what to do, I head to the goal, which is a parking space marked with two jackets in bundles on the ground. The rest of them finish picking teams, and the game starts.

We are the better team. Our players are always clustered around the opposing team's goal trying to score. All of a sudden, someone from the other team gets the ball and heads toward me, his teammates yelling at him. To be safe, I come forward. It's not a very good kick, but I almost miss the ball because I don't see it right away. They'll kill me if it goes in the goal. Luckily, I manage to grab it and quickly kick it away.

Filippo cheats. He kicks and elbows people and never lets his teammates have the ball. I can tell because wherever he goes, all the players around him either end up on the ground or yelling "Foul!" at him. One of my teammates goes straight for him, and it gets a bit confusing. After a bit I realize Kevin has scored because our team is shouting and running all over the field with their shirts on their heads like real soccer players. I do it too, with my sweater. It gets tangled in my glasses, but who cares.

Play resumes right away, and I've hardly had time to put my sweater back on over my shirt when Filippo comes dribbling down the field, the ball glued to his feet. It's just me between him and the goal. I'm really sweating, and my glasses start to steam up. I'm not crying, it's the heat, but I can't make out what's happening. I get ready to block. For a second I catch sight of Filippo's leg, pulling back to kick the ball while still running, and then something whacks my left shoulder and I hear the ball bounce near me. I try not to think about the pain and to catch the ball in my hands, but all I can see is something white floating between me and the goal. I touch it. The other team shrieks, "Own goal!" and runs about wildly, just like we did.

My teammates come over. They're furious, they're talking over each other, but I . . . I really didn't see the ball coming.

Maybe I should stop playing.

I head over to my parents' car, if it's where I think it is. No one tries to stop me. I don't even bother to say goodbye to Chiara. Behind me I hear Filippo call out to the others, "Come on, let's start again. Who wants to be in the goal?"

* * *

Cosimo, why won't you help me?

You liked playing with the children in Ombrosa, even though they were actually petty thieves and your job was to be the lookout from the branches of the tree. See, everyone has a friend to help them. I only have Ottimo Turcaret, who can't speak and is probably really bad at soccer. It's only fair you help me because you have the child thieves, Viola, and a brother. I don't have any of these, and if you don't help me, I'll make your brother disappear from the book with the power of my mind and be born to me instead, although I'm not sure how to make a brother be born.

Come to think of it, are you there with my grandma? Does she live in the tree with the giant after they cut down her cherry tree? That would mean you have a grandma to spend time with now too. Well, I think you should ask her to send me a signal, a thump, anything. A special anything. If you don't, I won't believe she's there or that you're really trying to help me.

Cosimo, promise you'll help me?

7

Playing Soccer with the Boys

W hat's wrong with you?"

Estella looks out at me from the janitor's office, the one in the entrance hall, and for a second her eyes scare me again.

"Nothing. Why?"

"You have the face of someone whose cat just die."

"Ottimo Turcaret is just fine, thanks."

Estella is not on good terms with Ottimo Turcaret because she's convinced he does his business in the organic vegetable garden when he waits for me after school. She might not like my cat, but she always notices when I'm upset. She has a third eye too.

"So, what happened?"

I go into the room, sit on the swivel chair, and spin myself around with my feet.

"Nothing. Just that I keep messing things up."

Estella tells me to get off the chair. She sits down on it and rummages around in the bottom of a drawer, hunting for the bags of extra-crunchy chips she hides in her desk. She offers me a packet and we munch on them together.

"You are messy, Mafalda, that's just who you are."

I stop eating for a second and look at my feet. "No, it's not that. It's because I can't see."

She holds up a chip in front of me. "How many can you see?"

"One."

"There, you can see."

I throw away my bag into the trash can under the desk as I struggle to hold back the tears.

"Who cares how many chips I can see? I want to play soccer. I want to be able to see the ball when it comes."

"And I want to go to the moon tomorrow morning."

I could punch her on the nose when she does that. But then she smiles with those bright pink lips, and I feel like laughing too, as I imagine her not coming to school tomorrow and ringing me to say she's on the moon.

She also stops eating. "Mafalda, it's not important to be able to see everything, you know?"

"Of course it is! I need to see the ball if I'm going to play soccer."

"Is playing soccer really that important to you?"

"Yes, it really, really is."

"So much you'd die if you didn't play?"

I think for a moment. "Hmm, maybe not that much."

"It's not essential then."

Estella throws away the empty chip packet.

"What do you mean by 'essential'?"

She wipes her hands on a paper towel, then picks up her bag and pulls out a small book. She flicks through it and signals to me to come over the way she always does, with a quick opening and closing of her hand. I stand behind her and try to read it, but I can't. The words in books are too small for me, like tiny black ants sitting on the page saying nothing.

"What is it?"

Estella reads aloud.

"'Goodbye,' said the fox. 'And now here is my secret, a very simple secret. It is only with the heart that one can see rightly; what is essential is invisible to the eye.'"

"It's *The Little Prince*!"

"Correct. You didn't read the words, but you know what book it is."

"But what's that got to do with me? I don't know what essential is."

"Do you remember what was essential for the Little Prince?"

"His rose, I think."

"Could he see it?"

"No, because he'd left it behind on his planet."

We sit in silence for a bit. I wait for her to explain it better. She doesn't. She stands up, puts her hands on my shoulders, and says, "Find your rose, Mafalda. The thing that's essential to you. Something you can do, even without your eyes."

She spins me round till I'm facing the hallway and pushes me out. Then shuts the door. From behind the door, I hear her start to sing a song by Marco Mengoni. It's a sign for me to go, and I realize I'm super late for my next class. Thanks, Estella.

I'm nearly at the end of the corridor when I hear the door open and she yells, "Never throw food in the trash! Next time you pick it out and take home to ugly cat!"

* * *

Something I don't need my eyes to do. I'm lying on the bed with my notebook open on my knees, Ottimo Turcaret warming my feet.

It's not easy. You can't do much without eyes. It's not fair. Why did Stargardt mist have to happen to me?

I draw a line through *Playing soccer*, toss the notebook under the bed, and switch off the light.

The cherry tree had chestnut hair with yellow streaks like Mom this morning.

One hundred and twenty steps.

There are sixty meters between my eyes and the cherry tree.

Part Three

Fifty Meters

8

Not Being Alone

I'm really good at bandaged man's buff.

I know the game's not really called that, but I don't like the other word—"blind." I prefer "bandaged" because you're in the dark only while you're playing the game. I'd like to have a dream about playing bandaged man's buff, wake up, and realize I've still got the bandage on so I could take it off and see clearly again.

No one ever wants to play bandaged man's buff with me. They think I'm cheating because I always find them, even when my eyes are blindfolded. I have a secret tactic—I stand right in the middle and listen for someone moving. It's so easy to catch people when they move—you just run to where the noise is coming from. No one expects it. After a while they get angry, saying that I must be able to see from under the blindfold, and get the Dragon Ball cards out. I couldn't cheat at Dragon Ball even if I wanted to. I can't read the cards.

So I'm playing by myself in the garden. Mom lets me stay here while she takes a shower, but she wants me to be back by the time she's dry. Mom is superfast in the shower and doesn't even use the hair dryer so she can get back to watching me as quickly as she can. This means I can stay outside by myself for eight or nine minutes, more or less. I'm using a fluffy scarf I took from her wardrobe—a dark one—and tied it over my eyes so I can't even see out by mistake. My plan is to go from the toolshed to the fence on the other side of the garden without stopping and without stretching my arms out in front of me like a zombie.

I've no idea why I play this game, but I want to know what it feels like to walk in the dark. It was really scary the first few times I tried, and I pulled the blindfold off after just a couple of teeny-weeny steps. I can do it easily now. Walking in the dark is weird, like swimming through the black, liquid leaves of trees whose branches reach out to stop you—in a kind way, not ripping your T-shirt. You keep going, feeling the danger, but also balancing alone, as if someone you don't know is watching you and not your mom on the balcony.

Grandma used to say you have to try things to understand them. So, I'm trying.

My fingers brush against the dry hydrangea shrubs along the garden wall. I stick close to them so I don't wander into the middle of the garden. I always go the wrong way when I walk with my eyes shut, even when I think I'm going straight. I've only taken a few steps when something fluffy rubs past my legs and gets in the way—Ottimo Turcaret. I have to stop so I don't step on him, and to pet him too. I pick him up and walk to the bottom of the garden, Ottimo Turcaret purring against my chest. He's warm and heavy. If I didn't know he was gray, I'd swear he was one of those big fat ginger cats with a huge head and a fat neck. Cats with ginger coats are rounder than the others. I wonder why.

My toe touches the wooden fence and I stop. While I'm deciding whether to turn around and go back or continue along the fence, I hear a bicycle brake squeal very near me, probably someone in the parking garage behind our block of apartments.

"Hi."

I whip my blindfold off. The afternoon light flashes
stars in front of my eyes, but I put my glasses back on
as quickly as I can. I see Filippo in his blue jacket, sitting on what looks like a girls' bike, a yellow one with
no basket. He has his hands on his hips, fists clenched,
legs apart, and he's on his tiptoes so he won't fall off the
bike that probably belongs to someone else—maybe
his sister or his mom. He's wearing the same jacket as
on All Saints' Day, even though that was a month ago
and it's much colder now. He must really like having
his name written on the back. It means everyone rec-
ognizes him and knows who he is.

I'd like to go back in and not have to speak to him.
I'm scared he'll hit me the way he does with everyone
else, although I'd stick up for myself. I pull Ottimo
Turcaret closer. I don't think he'd protect me in a fight.
Dogs do that. Cats are opportunists. And they don't
know how to come down cherry trees.

"Do you know why cats can't come down cherry
trees?" The question just tumbles out before I realize
it. Grandma always said there was no such thing as a
stupid question, although I feel a bit stupid now.

"What?" Filippo puts his hands on the handlebars
and pulls the brakes even though he's not moving. He
seems taken aback by the question.

"Forget it."

"Do you live here?"

"You don't even know who I am."

"Yes, I do. You're the girl from the soccer game."

"My name's Mafalda."

"And I'm Filippo."

I put Ottimo Turcaret down. "I know."

Filippo leans forward, still sitting on the bike, and puts a hand through the railings to stroke Ottimo Turcaret. I'm a bit nervous because I'm scared he'll hurt him. But Filippo rubs behind the ears and Ottimo Turcaret seems to like it.

"What's he called?"

"Ottimo Turcaret."

"Your cat has a last name?"

"It's a double-barreled name. From a book."

"Really? What book?"

"You won't know it. It's for grown-ups. It's my dad's favorite book."

"My dad likes reading too. He always used to read me a story at bedtime."

"Mine does too." It doesn't seem polite to ask why he said "used to." Maybe his mom and dad are divorced and his dad doesn't live with them anymore. Usually people whose parents are divorced get really upset if you ask them. So, I don't say anything.

"Which book is it, then?"

"What book?"

"Your dad's favorite."

I don't want to tell him, but his fists are clenched on his hips again and I'm a little scared. "*The Baron in the Trees.*"

"Have you read it?"

I don't understand why he's so interested.

"Yes. My dad read it to me."

"That means he read it, not you."

"It's the same thing."

Filippo puts his elbows on the fence and rests his chin in his hands. "Did he read it to you because you're blind?"

I feel my face go red and my glasses steam up. "I'm not blind." I lift up Ottimo Turcaret to go home, but Mom's scarf falls to the ground and I have trouble finding it.

"But you can't see much, can you?"

I ignore him and keep looking for the scarf, feeling the cold, dry grass with my free hand. In the end I decide to give up and just go home.

I turn my back on Filippo. That was mean of him—I didn't ask him if his mom and dad are divorced. I hear a clatter of pedals and bicycle chain, then a thud and his feet coming up beside mine on the dry grass in the garden. "Go away," I say without turning round.

"Here."

When someone says "here," it usually means they're giving you something, so I reach into the mist and my hand touches something silky soft. The scarf.

"Mafalda!"

Mom's worried voice reaches me from the French doors. I think more than eight or nine minutes must have gone past since Mom went into the shower. My instinct is to run straight for the front door, but I remember that when someone picks something up from the ground for you, something you couldn't find and that wasn't yours to begin with, something you took without asking, you're supposed to say thanks.

I stop on the path and see a fuzzy blue blob disappearing into the distance.

I don't feel like shouting "thank you," not with Mom watching me from the balcony.

"Come inside!"

I go in. As the door closes behind me, I hear a bike in the street outside, trilling its bell cheerily, and the *ting-ting* continues until the sound is too small even for me to hear. I can only imagine where the bell's owner can be going; he sounds so happy and free. I'd like to ask him to come back, to give me a ride on the back of his bike, because I haven't been fast on a bike for such a long time, or on foot, for that matter. But he's free; he has clear glasses and can go wherever he wants. Not me. I'm in prison, as if the police have put me in jail but the bars are made of fog and all my cellmates have already escaped.

I'm in my room, still in my bathrobe, lying on the bed. I reach over for my personal organizer and open it to the second page, the one with the important things on it. I draw a black line through *Not being alone*.

I found a note, folded in four, on my desk at school this morning.

I thought it was a white butterfly when I first saw it, but thinking about it, that would be impossible. It's too cold for butterflies now—they've all gone away on vacation or to a tree trunk like Grandma and her giant.

I never get notes. Whenever the teacher turns to write on the board, the people in my class start throwing notes around. I don't know what they say—they don't throw them to me. I sit in the front row, otherwise I wouldn't be able to read anything on the board and I'd miss all the homework, but I still hear the paper flying around behind me. Every now and then, one will hit my back and fall to the ground with a *phut*. When I turned round to pick one up once, the teacher saw me. She shouted because she thought I'd written the note. Everyone laughed, so I decided to forget about the notes.

This one was just for me, waiting on my desk like a butterfly poised delicately on a flower. I went into the bathroom to read it in private. I don't want my classmates to see me reading—that would be embarrassing. I need to get my face so close to the paper, even to read the really big writing; I'm like old people at the supermarket who can't see the sell-by date on the bags of salad. But I'm not old; I'm ten. Dad bought me a magnifying glass. He says I could use it like Sherlock Holmes, the detective we often read about in Dad's books and sometimes see in movies. I would never ever use it in front of other people.

That's why I go into the girls' bathroom—note in one pocket, magnifying glass in the other—and lock myself in.

I open the note. It says: *You go all red when you answer questions. You are my little princess, or better, my baroness.*

9

Playing My Pavement Game Where if You Fall off the Lines, You End Up in the Lava and Die

The school cherry tree is awfully sad in winter.

The leaves go away on vacation with the butterflies, and the giant inside the tree takes the flowers off the branches to make them into a colored blanket.

Without its beautiful foliage, I can't see it from very far away. Luckily, I know I'm almost there when I hear Estella's whistle, although Dad would tell me anyway. In the past I was too young to come to school by myself, and now that I have Stargardt mist, I'll never be allowed out without an adult.

If Ottimo Turcaret were a dog, like Cosimo's

dachshund in the book (although it wasn't really his; it was Viola's), he could guide me. I would have to train him because he's not the cleverest cat. It doesn't matter, though; I love him just as much because he waits for me outside school and no one else has a cat that waits for them outside school.

When the bell rings at the end of the day, we're supposed to wait in line, but my class is all over the place and the teacher can never check if we've left with the right parents. Estella usually takes me to the gate—my parents asked her to. But she's not here today. I go into the janitor's office to ask if they know where she is, and the other one, the one with no hair whose T-shirt is always splashed with pasta sauce, tells me she left early for a checkup. I wonder what she needed to check. He doesn't bother to ask me if I need help walking to the gate. This janitor always shuts himself away in the office, making coffee, and he couldn't care less about the children, except when they get sick. That's only because he has to clean it up.

I go out of school and stop just outside the gate. Mom and Dad want me to wait here. They're sometimes a few minutes late because they both work in another town and have to rush over by car to pick me up on time.

There's hardly anyone around. The bus has gone; the cars of all the other parents are leaving. Some children go past on bikes, and amid the shouting and squealing, I think I hear a bell that I recognize. When he emerges from the group, or rather the mishmash of colors moving in unison along the white line on the pavement, I recognize the noise of the brakes and the blue jacket.

"Hi."

"Hi."

"Are you waiting for your mom and dad?"

Something soft passes through my legs the way it did the other day. I lift up Ottimo Turcaret and, on the spur of the moment, decide to start walking home.

"No. I was waiting for him."

Filippo strokes Ottimo Turcaret's head as I go past him, but I soon leave him behind as I head away as fast as I can along the street. Mom will be furious when she arrives and can't find me. She'll think I've been kidnapped, but I keep walking anyway. I want Filippo to think I'm going home alone and that I do it every day. I have to look relaxed. If Mom or Dad appear now, I'll get into so much trouble and look like an idiot in front of Filippo. So instead of going straight, I turn down the first street on the right then turn again into another street.

I hear Filippo's bike braking near me again.

"Which way are you going?" he asks, pedaling slowly.

I'd forgotten he knows where I live. I blush and don't answer.

"If you ask me, you're going to get lost. I'll take you."

"No, thanks."

I don't know why he's following me. Maybe he wants to steal Ottimo Turcaret. He seems to like him a lot. I need to turn off this street and get rid of him. But I've stopped paying attention and now I don't know where to go. I try to read the street name, but all I can see are ants where the words should be.

Filippo is still behind me.

"I told you you'd get lost. Come on, I'll take you."

"No."

"Don't you want to go home?"

"No. I want to go for a walk."

The make-up-pathways-on-the-pavement game comes to mind. I walk over to the edge of the pavement and start playing.

Filippo follows me. "What are you doing?"

"Playing a game."

"What game?"

"You have to walk along a line, and if you fall off, you end up in the lava and crocodiles eat you."

"There are crocodiles in the lava? How do they survive?"

"It doesn't matter. It's made up. But if you fall off, you lose."

"How long do you have to keep it up?"

"I don't know. As long as you can."

"What a stupid game."

Filippo jumps on the pedals and scoots away without saying goodbye.

There you go, I've embarrassed myself and I'm lost. To be on the safe side, I keep playing weird pathways because I think I can still hear Filippo's bike, and if he comes back, it has to look like I really am just hanging out.

I get home almost by mistake, and an hour has passed since school finished. This is another thing I can do, count time in my head. Not that it's much help right now.

Mom is standing in the doorway of our building, cell phone at her ear. She runs toward me as soon as she sees me, falls to her knees, and hugs me so tight I can hardly breathe.

"We were worried to death. Thank goodness you're safe. What happened to you?"

Dad runs down from the stairs and scoops me into his strong arms.

I can't face telling them I walked home on my own, not right away. They're bound to shout at me. But they look so worried, so I tell a half-truth.

"I really wanted to come home on my own, but I got lost. Sorry, Mom."

I try to look concerned and sad. It usually works, but not this time. Dad starts shouting, "We've told you a million times to wait outside the school! You can't come home on your own, you know that."

Mom lays a hand on his arm and says, "John." Mom always does this when something serious happens that makes Dad angry. She calms him down. Other times she calls him "J, darling." Dad goes back upstairs, stamping his feet on each step, muttering to himself. We go up too, and by the time we reach our landing, I can smell pepperoni pizza, my favorite. Mom takes me into the kitchen and gives me a huge slice even though I worried her to death. She also gives Dad one. He doesn't say thank you, but he lays a hand on her arm as she leans over his plate with the pizza, and looks at her. At moments like these, I think that Mom and Dad could almost be friends.

It's evening. I put on my blue pajamas and pick up Ottimo Turcaret. I go over to my bedroom window, but I don't put Ottimo Turcaret on the window ledge so he doesn't get cold. I look out.

For a second my heart skips a beat, then starts hammering under the soft fabric of my pajamas. I can't see the North Star. The moon's there, right in front of me, shining like a streetlamp, but the star that's usually beside it is not. I can't make it out. I want to shout for Mom, tell her that Jesus's match has gone out, but I decide to say nothing. I screw up my eyes, close one, then the other. Nothing. The dark blue sky looks clean and smooth and cloudless. The only clouds are in my eyes, and they've covered the North Star. For Christmas, I'll ask for one of those lamps that projects stars onto the ceiling; that way I'll still be able to see some—five or six, maybe even fourteen or fifteen, since they'll be closer than the sky. Meanwhile, I know what I have to do. I get my personal organizer out, turn to the right page, and draw a black line through *Playing my pavement game where if you fall off the lines, you end up in the lava and die.*

Cosimo, when are you going to give me a hand?

It almost felt like you were helping me these past few days, I'm not sure why. But then something bad always happens, and I realize you're not with me; you're playing chess on a branch with my grandma, fur hat on your head, not giving me a second thought. You're all nice and cozy in your fur hat, whereas I'm running from monsters in the dark. If they catch me, they'll eat me up, and what am I supposed to do then? Will you tell me, Cosimo?

When Does the Struggle End?

Christmas.

It's raining. Yuck.

I can hear the rain clearly. The noise is so loud, it drowns out everything else. I'm standing by my bedroom window, breathing on the glass to make it steam up. I draw a star with my finger. The glass is cold against my forehead. I feel like I'm in another world where the rain is drumming on my heart.

I don't hear Mom shout to me to open my presents. It's only when she lays a hand on my shoulder and says it's time that I realize. I also remember I didn't ask someone to give me a star-projector light.

It's morning, late, and it will soon be time to put on my red-and-white checkered dress, the one that gives you sore eyes. We're going to lunch at my aunt and uncle's house. Thank goodness Cousin Andrea will be there with Ravina, his girlfriend with the third eye. At least I'll have some fun with them. I don't look at the dress laid out flat on my bed, and I follow Mom into the living room.

Miraculously, our Christmas tree is still alive. Mom and Dad are not very good with plants. We put the spruce near the French windows so it would be in the light, but the needles are already so dry, even the lighter-than-light glass balls are starting to drop off. The woman at the shop at the mall said it would last until spring. Ottimo Turcaret wasn't supposed to wee in the pot, though. I didn't see him do it, but I can smell it.

I sit on the rug near the tree and sniff the presents. I think they're safe. Dad put them under the lowest branches late last night when he thought I was sleeping. How am I supposed to sleep when Santa Claus is coming? The really wonderful thing about Christmas, though, is that it comes for everyone. Even for people like me who can't see anything but the moon without their glasses.

Mom puts her present in my hands. It's a tiny

parcel wrapped in gold paper, perfect, with a red ribbon all round it. Inside there's an iPod with earphones to listen to music.

"I've put all your favorite songs on it."

It's a lovely present. I wasn't expecting it.

"Can I put books on it too?"

Mom looks at Dad. He kneels down beside me on the rug. "How do you know there are books you can listen to?"

"The special-needs teacher told me."

Dad strokes my head the way I do with Ottimo Turcaret. It feels quite nice. "What books would you like?"

I look at him, nudging my glasses up my nose with my index finger. "Your favorite."

Dad smiles. "Okay. Give me a couple of days. I'll download it for you."

Then he gives me his present. It's bigger than Mom's, and soft. I take my time unwrapping it. I hope it's not a sweater. When relatives give you clothes, they always get the size wrong and usually think you like a color that you actually hate. But you can't say anything—that would be rude. Then whenever you go to see them, you have to wear the sweater you don't like.

This isn't a sweater, though. I pull a big, colorful blanket out of the wrapping paper and spread it out on my knees. It's made of knitted squares, stitched together into a blanket, in loads of different colors—yellow, bright pink, green. All beautiful, bold colors. I run my hand over it. The wool doesn't scratch like wonky sweaters; it's silky and smooth. I feel like wrapping the blanket round me and lying on the rug to listen to the rain.

What a strange present from Dad. I think he notices I'm surprised because he sits down beside me and explains that the blanket was a gift from Grandma for my eleventh birthday. To finish all the pieces in time, she worked on it late at night. She started it not long before she went into the hospital. "Do you remember when we drove her there?"

I bury my face in the blanket so Dad can't see my eyes. "Yes." Then a thought comes to me. "Why didn't she just do eight pieces? It would've been quicker. I turned eight the year she went to live in the tree."

"She liked surprises. She didn't want to blow it all on your eighth birthday. She wanted you to have something to remember her by later."

"Did she want to come back?"

"Sort of."

I feel happy. So happy I forget to give my presents to Mom and Dad. I'd only made them drawings of their faces, portraits I worked on in secret, copied very carefully from their wedding photo in the silver frame in the hallway. I'll put them on their pillows tonight.

Before I start getting ready for lunch, something occurs to me.

"If this was meant as a birthday present, why are you giving it to me now?"

Mom and Dad catch each other's eye. Mom replies, "We thought we'd bring the surprise forward a few months. We couldn't hide the blanket any longer; it was too exciting."

They remain by my side, silent, for a few minutes, then exchange their own presents. I'd like to tell them I understand, that they did the right thing giving me the beautiful blanket now. While I can still see it. I pull the blanket around my shoulders, holding it tight.

Ravina is beautiful today. She has her hair in a side braid that reaches down to her waist, and she has blue eye shadow. She's wearing a fancy dress, though not an Indian one, and even though she's not our religion, she smells of church. She always smells of church because she reminds me of the white smoke the priest sprinkles over people during mass. When she sees me, she gives me an enormous hug and then her present, which is a poster of a flamingo and a frog.

The frog is in the flamingo's mouth, but it hasn't been eaten yet because it has its hands round the flamingo's neck. You can tell from the flamingo's face that it wants to swallow the frog but can't because of the hands round its neck. The words NEVER EVER GIVE UP are written below the picture. I ask Ravina about it.

"It's telling you to hang on, whatever it takes. Just like the frog."

I start to giggle. "He's definitely in for it!"

Ravina taps me on the nose. "Not yet, Mafalda. Not yet."

"So, when does the struggle end?"

"When one of the two gives up."

"Who do you think will give up first?"

Ravina looks at the poster for a few seconds.

"It doesn't matter. The important thing is to never ever give up."

I move closer to the poster to get a better look. The frog looks really uncomfortable. His head is right inside the flamingo's beak, and his back legs are dangling in midair.

"Okay, but it looks like hard work."

"Well, would you rather be chewed and swallowed?"

"No! That's disgusting!"

"Soooo . . ."

"Never ever give up. I get it. Thanks. I'll put it up in my room when I get home."

11

I Know!

Mom only puts high heels on twice a year, apart from when she takes me to the doctor. She wears them on her and Dad's wedding anniversary, which they usually celebrate at home with a special meal that she cooks, and on New Year's Eve, which is today.

I hear her tip-tapping around the kitchen, laying out glasses and the snacks she has just made with Dad. They gave me a sparkling apple cider, then sent me to my room to get changed. Mom has left me out two sparkly hair ribbons and some of her perfume—it's too strong for me, but I like it because it's hers.

Standing in front of the mirror in my bedroom, trying to bury the sparkly ribbons in my hair, I realize that Mom and Dad are talking about something they don't want me to hear—they've lowered their voices and are whispering to each other. I want to eavesdrop, although I know I'm not supposed to. I tiptoe silently over to the door. Mom's heels are still tapping around the kitchen. I listen hard to pick up what she's saying and understand why she's speaking so quietly.

"It'll be difficult at first."

A chair scrapes on the floor. Dad must have stood up. "Are you sure you want to do this?"

"Yes. We have no choice."

"Can't you just take leave?"

"Why bother? Things are only going to get worse. I'll have to be with her all day."

That will be me.

I hear them sigh, standing still. There can't be any more dishes to sort.

"Have you spoken to your boss yet?"

"I mentioned it. He says he can't change my hours because I already have permission to be absent for Mafalda's appointments. He suggested I hand in my notice and he'll give me a decent payoff."

Her notice? What does that mean?

"Let's hope so. When would you stop?"

"First of February."

"Okay. Maybe it's for the best. I'll take extra hours at work. We also need to start thinking about the house."

I don't understand. My head fills up with worrying thoughts, like the white butterflies that flutter around the cherry tree.

"The agency has given me some contacts. On Monday we start viewing apartments beside the school."

"Did you explain we can't have stairs?"

"Yes. And that we have a limited budget."

A sneeze squeezes out—I can't stop it in time— and everything goes quiet in the kitchen. The whole house falls quiet for a second.

"Mafalda, are you ready?"

I go into the hallway. "Yes, Mom."

"Let's go, then."

It's a quarter to one in the morning, and I'm sleeping in my aunt and uncle's bed while the grown-ups drink from tiny glasses and speak in hushed tones in the living room.

I'm not actually asleep. I keep thinking about the conversation I overheard earlier. If they're seriously thinking about moving to a new house, what happens to me? What will I do if we get a house where I can't see the moon from my bedroom window? And I wouldn't be able to see Grandma's house anymore, even though the new neighbors who never say hello live there now. And what about Ottimo Turcaret? What if he doesn't like the new house? He's used to this one, and I don't know if he'll want to move somewhere else.

I have to do something. My backpack with my clothes for tomorrow is sitting by the bed. It's also got my pencil case, some paper to draw on, and the iPod Mom gave me for Christmas. I feel around for the iPod in the dark, put my earphones in, and press the round play button. I'm listening to Dad's favorite book. The story resumes in the powerful voice of a man who sounds old.

> *"Where are you going?"*
>   *Through the glass door we saw him in the hall, picking up his three-cornered hat and his small sword.*
>   *"I know!" He ran into the garden.*
> *Shortly afterward, through the windows, we saw him climbing up the holm oak.*

I press stop and sit up with a jolt. I know what to do. I'll go and live in a tree, like Cosimo. If I move to the school cherry tree, I can watch lessons through the window and no one will see me hidden in the branches.

I need to get organized because I'll be in the dark soon and I won't be able to go up and down the tree with all the things I need. I should make a plan. I get a sheet of paper and my pencil out of my backpack and start playing the old man's voice again.

He was dressed and coiffed with great propriety, as our father wanted him to come to the table, thougwh he was only twelve: hair powdered and ponytail tied with a ribbon . . .

I make a note on my list to look up what "powdered" means, but at least I have a ribbon. So, what's next?

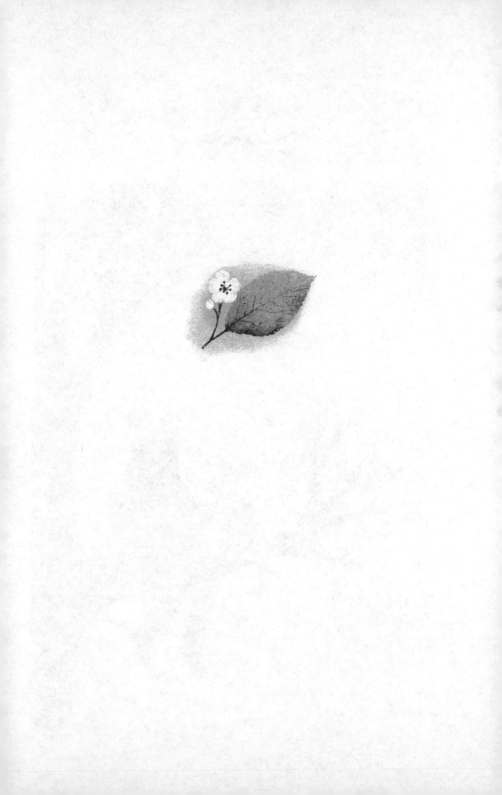

Part Four

Forty Meters

12

See What My Face Is Like When I'm Grown-Up

A saucepan to cook food in.

    A mattress to sleep more comfortably.

iPod.

Grandma's blanket.

Pens, notebooks, pencils.

A big umbrella to stay dry.

A—

"Mafalda, what are you doing?"

I slip the list of things to take up the tree into my notebook. The teacher sees me. I'm in the front row, right beside her desk, but she pretends not to. She tells me to pay attention and nothing more.

I pick up the dinosaur pencil Doctor Olga gave me and pretend I'm going to write something, and the teacher turns back toward the board.

"So, there are two types of muscles—long and short. . . ."

Muscles. Who cares if they are long and short? I stop listening immediately but keep looking so the teacher doesn't suspect anything, secretly going over the list in my head as she speaks.

A saucepan to cook food in.

Ah, I still haven't thought about where I'll get food once I'm in the tree. I could bring a few supplies to begin with. Then there's the problem of the bed. I need a blow-up mattress to lay over two adjacent branches. Chiara has a double one. Her mom and dad took it to the lake the last time we went on a day out, all of us together with our moms and dads. That was a long time ago, but they should still have it. Or maybe they'll have bought a new one. They are quite well-off. I wonder if Chiara would lend it to me. Probably not. We aren't that close anymore. I'll have to borrow it without asking. Didn't Robin Hood do that? He stole from the rich to give to the poor. Chiara is rich, and it's as if I'm poor, now that I have to go and live in the tree by myself. If I were older, I could buy all this stuff with my own money, but if I wait until I'm big enough, it might be too late, as the dark in my eyes is getting bigger much faster than I am.

I look around to see who else in my class is rich enough for me to borrow something without asking. This means turning to look behind me, but the teacher is busy drawing muscles in red chalk. My classmates don't notice that I'm spying on them—they're all busy drawing too, although I bet they're not copying muscles from the board. Kevin, who sits behind me, is holding a green pencil, so he's definitely drawing snakes. He's crazy about them, and I know he'd like to have one but hasn't got the money to buy one. He's not rich.

I'm not sure what's happening at the back of the class, but there's a lot of fidgeting and agitation, I can feel it. I think Chiara and Martina are playing truth or dare with the boys in front of them, Christian and Lorenzo, and everyone around them is giggling. Christian is rich. He has a swimming pool, and every year he gets a new backpack for school. On school trips, he always brings a fancy pack that unfolds into a poncho when it rains. That would be useful.

There's a massive "Aaa-choo!" in the row by the window.

"Ugh! You sneezed all over my notebook!" I hear

Francesca exclaim. She's a friend of mine who moved from Sicily this year. Poor her, she's right. She has Rory, whose nickname is Roly, sitting next to her. He's not very tall and is round and pink, like a beach ball. He never stops eating, even when it's not break time. There are bits of bread, lettuce, and mayonnaise sprayed all over his and Francesca's notebooks. Even I can see them—it was some sneeze.

The teacher goes over to her desk and asks Roly to clean it up. She yells at him for eating during class, and he pulls a pretty box out from under his desk. It must be a food container. I've seen something like it before—it keeps food warm. Dad has a green one that he uses to take his lunch to work. If I had one, I wouldn't have to worry about heating up my food in the tree. But I can't take Dad's; he needs it.

I'll have to take Roly's, which makes me feel bad because he's not very rich. The teacher is still busy sorting out Roly's splatter. Good. I pull out the sheet of paper hidden in my notebook, the one with the list on it, and write down everything I've decided this morning.

We're packing our bags to go home. There's a knock at the door, and Estella comes in with a letter.

She wouldn't tell me what checkup she had last month, the day she didn't come to school. "You don't need to know," she'd snapped. Then, when she saw I was staring at her, she added, "The dentist. Too many crunchy chips." That made me smile, and when she and I start laughing, it's impossible to go back to being serious.

"Children, listen up a second, please—this is about your school trip. You have to write the time and place you'll be leaving in your agendas." I'd forgotten that next week we were going on a skiing trip. This could be a stroke of luck for me because everyone will have the things that I need with them. The teacher dictates the details, and I doodle the words randomly in my agenda—I'm so distracted by my Robin Hood adventure. Estella, who's waiting for the teacher to sign a copy of the letter, looks at me and shakes her head. She leans over my desk and murmurs, "Come to my room after, and I'll stick the letter into your notebook."

So I go to Estella's room.

I always go, even though she's often in a sulk, or wants to scrunch me up like a sock, throw me in the washing machine, and give me a spin. That's probably why I go back to her, because she never pretends. Mom and Dad do. The teachers do, and the children in my class do. Only Estella and Ottimo Turcaret tell the truth, and that's important to me. Or maybe I like being with Estella because of the stories she tells me.

We're reading a book called *Heart* this month. She

says it's a bit sappy, but I love the character Garrone, especially when he takes the blame for someone else and the teacher can tell purely by looking in his eyes. *It wasn't you*, the teacher says to him, and Garrone goes back to his desk, sad, but he did a wonderful thing. I throw my bag under the desk in the janitors' room and sink into the swivel chair. To start spinning, I push against the desk, and my fingertips brush against *Heart*. I pick it up and bring it close to my face as I spin round. Since there's no one around except Estella, who's photocopying the letter about the school trip, I dig my magnifying glass out of my pocket and use it to read the author's name. Edmondo De Amicis. An Italian writer. I'd forgotten.

Estella rummages in my bag for my notebook, opens it at the right page, and slams it down in front of me, along with a glue stick. "Stick it in yourself. You know how to do it."

I start rolling the glue onto the page and peer at her from behind my glasses. "Estella, are there any writers in Romania?"

"Romanian writers? Of course there are. Why shouldn't there be?"

"Why do we never read Romanian stories?"

She smiles a bright pink smile that makes me happy I came to the janitors' room.

"Do you know the most famous Romanian story in the world? It's the story of Dracula."

I spring to my feet and the chair keeps spinning. "Dracula? Was Dracula from Romania? I thought he was English!"

Estella sits down and crosses her hands over her knees with an impish look that gives me the shivers— happy shivers. I love horror stories.

"He's not English. He's from Transylvania, in Romania. His name means "son of the devil." My grandma used to read it to me as a child, and it would terrify me. But I loved it at the same time."

I kneel down in front of her and she starts laughing. "Please, Estella, will you read it to me like your grandma did? Pretty please!"

"Do you like horror stories too?"

"Yes!"

"Why?"

"I don't know. Why did you like them?"

"Because if I could feel fear, it meant I was alive."

"Same here," I reply, although I don't really understand.

Estella can't keep me at school any longer. She looks out of the window and sees Mom's car. "Time's up today," she says, shoving my bag under my arm. "Another day. Ah, Mafalda . . ."

We stop at the door. Estella squeezes my hand.

"I wanted to ask you if you've thought about your essential thing?" I look at the ground. I hear her bending down to look me in the eye. "You have to think about it. It's important."

"Okay. Can I tell you some other time?"

We go down the steps. I see a red cloud outside the gates—Mom's car—and Estella lets go of my hand. "Yes, on you go. You've still got two or three months to decide."

I get into the car. Mom starts chatting right away, but I think about what Estella has just said. I don't have long, she's right. But even if that's true, and I like her to tell the truth, I sometimes wish she could be a little less truthful.

But time *is* running out.

Dad's home. He came back to have lunch with Mom and me, and to do something else. "We have a surprise for you," they announce, all touchy-feely and smiley. I squeeze Ottimo Turcaret and pop some tuna into his mouth. (I hate the stuff.) Dad stops being smiley and shouts at me. I wonder if maybe Dad hasn't read his favorite book lately because if he'd read it last night, for example, he'd know that you can't force children to eat things they don't like, otherwise they'll run away to trees, like Cosimo did when he didn't want to eat snails.

I put some tuna in my mouth, don't swallow it, and stare at Dad. There's a fuzzy aura around the edge of his head, like most things when I look at them for more than a few seconds, and I imagine Dad with a long, curly wig instead of his normal hair. I'm about to laugh, but then I think that my dad and Cosimo's dad, the baron, look very alike.

I'd like to do my homework as soon as I get home, so I can work on my secret plan to run away to the cherry tree, but Mom calls me into the bathroom, puts extra-tight pigtails in my hair, and tells me that we have to go somewhere. They end up taking me to see an apartment, much smaller than our house, on the ground floor, with a minuscule garden and no stairs (like Dad wanted). In the small room I bet they want to give me, I look out the window and all I can see is the wall of another house. The kitchen is gorgeous, all shiny with a new oven and dishwasher, but you can hear the footsteps of the people upstairs, and there's a big sign on the door of the building that says NO PETS.

On the way home, Mom and Dad keep asking what I think of the house, but I refuse to answer. I'm now planning how to get away as quickly as possible. Dad shouts goodbye from the hallway—he has to go back to work. I go out to say bye, then return to my bedroom.

I look around like I did at school. Ottimo Turcaret is sleeping on Grandma's blanket, which is spread out on my bed. He's not actually sleeping, because when I turn to look at him, he raises his head, purrs, and waits to be cuddled, like always. Looking at him reminds me of a picture in a book that Mom and Dad used to read to me as a child—it showed two children running away from home, on a raft with a bundle tied to the end of a stick as a suitcase. I could use Grandma's blanket to make a bundle like that.

"Well done, Ottimo Turcaret!"

I pull the blanket out from under the cat, nearly dragging him off the bed, but he clings on and mews angrily. I lay the blanket on the floor. It's light enough to tie knots in but also strong enough to carry things inside. I start gathering up a few objects and place them in the center of the blanket. I think I'll hide it under the bed for now, so that when I've finished getting everything ready, I can tie it up with a knot and slip the bundle into my schoolbag the first chance I get. The stick is a good idea, but I'd be found out right away—who goes around with a stick on their shoulders? I'll pretend I'm going to school, and instead of my books, I'll put the things I need to live in the tree into my schoolbag. The perfect plan. I glance at the mirror to give myself a thumbs-up, but all I see is a shadow, and it seems a very long way away.

I get my notebook from the shelf above the bed and open it to the second page.

See what my face is like when I'm grown-up.

My glasses steam up and I can hardly see to cross out the words before everything goes cloudy in front of me, around me, and inside me.

> *Cosimo, why are you not helping me?*
>
> *I might have found a way to come and live with you and Grandma in the tree, but I need that really big something, remember? You traveled from tree to tree to get to the Spanish village, but what can I do? There aren't as many trees here as in Ombrosa. And I have to do everything by myself. It's my birthday soon, and I can already imagine the party I'd have if I lived in the cherry tree— the branches would be decked out in paper chains and balloons, and there would be one of Grandma's tarts, and loud music, the kind that makes your face tingle and your heart beat so hard you turn it up even louder.*
>
> *Will you help me organize it, Cosimo?*

13

Eat Black Olives, Sing in a Band

The midterm recital is on at the music school today, and I've come to hear Cousin Andrea and his guitar students play.

I love music. Maybe it's because there's nothing to see. Mom wanted me to learn to play an instrument, but I always said no, especially since I've had the mist in my eyes, because I can't read the notes. They look like ants sitting on a black line to me.

I like listening to music, though. When the lights go down in the theater, I close my eyes, and the guitar, the violin, and the piano music reach out to me, making my skin tingle, like walking really slowly on wet sand in the summer at around five o'clock in the afternoon when nothing bad can happen.

"There's that boy who comes to talk to you in the courtyard."

Mom's pointing to the stage. I sit up straight in my chair and try to get a better view.

"Who? Where is he?"

"The boy on the girl's bike. He's in the group of young pianists."

Filippo? Young pianists? It can't be him. Mom must have my mist in her eyes now too. We clap and the concert starts.

The nursery children sing first, the ones from the choir course. Then the violinists play. It's torture.

"There he is, that's him. What did you say his name is?"

I see someone walk onto the stage, stop for a second in the center under the big light, and then sit down at the huge, black piano.

"Filippo."

"Oh yes. It's written on his jacket as well."

So it is him.

A hush falls over the theater and Filippo begins to play. It must be a difficult song because it lasts a long time. I wish I could see his fingers because the beautiful music they're making is filling my head, taking my hand, and telling me to run with it, the way a friend would. So, I run, I run along a never-ending keyboard that turns into a beach, and the notes are waves. I jump over them, into them, like a dolphin now, free. The music commands the sea, making it move at its will. When I open my eyes, it has filled the whole room as far as the ceiling with rainbow-colored flowers, under the water and floating on the surface; then the music descends in limpid droplets, like the voice of the man reading the books on my iPod.

The silence when Filippo stops playing is immense. You can hear it. Then everyone starts to clap so loudly, the chairs vibrate. Filippo doesn't come to the edge of the stage to take a bow. He goes straight off, even though some people in the audience shout for an encore. Middle-school students with guitars come on after him, and Andrea gets them into position on the stage. The music Filippo played is stuck in my head, though, and I don't know if I'm more surprised he played it, or that there's something so beautiful in the world, it can make you cry.

Refreshments are served after the show. Mom and Dad lavish praise on Andrea and start chatting with him and Ravina near the sandwich table.

"Can I go and see the piano?"

Dad says no right away, but Mom touches his arm—"John"—and I'm allowed to wander away on my own.

I go into the theater. It's empty and the lights are off; only the black piano is lit up by a spotlight. "They're going to take it away now," someone sitting in the front row says. I didn't know he was there.

"I didn't know you were there."

Filippo stands up. "I know. Did I scare you?"

I go over to where he's sitting. "No. What are they going to take away?"

"The piano." Filippo puts a hand round my wrist and leads me onto the stage. We sit on the piano stool. "The school can't afford such a big piano, so every time we do a recital, a rich man lends us his."

"You play really well. I didn't know."

"Because I don't tell anyone. My dad forces me to play. I'm not that good."

I say nothing. Filippo runs the fingers of one hand along the black and white keys.

"He didn't even come to see me today."

"It wasn't because you're not good."

"What do you know about anything?"

I've made him angry. I try to say sorry. "Play something for me. The song from before."

"No." Filippo shuts the piano. "Weren't you

listening? I don't like studying piano; I only do it because I'm forced to."

"Even if you choose what you want to play?"

Filippo stops to think. "I taught myself a more modern song once. It's still kind of old, but not like the one I played earlier."

"Let's hear it."

"I'm not sure I remember it. I haven't got the music here."

"Just play."

Filippo lets out a little sigh and places his fingers on the keys but doesn't start playing right away. He turns to look at me. I look back and am about to ask what's wrong when he takes my hands and places them, palms flat, fingers spread open wide, on the piano, beside the little shelf where the music goes.

"Why?"

"Just keep them there."

He starts playing a song I've often heard Dad play. It talks about a yellow submarine. It's weird—before I even hear it with my ears, it feels like the sound is coming into my head through my hands, from the surface of the piano, which is like solid, slippery petroleum, warm below my skin. The notes run down Filippo's arms. I feel them move beside me, then move the surface of the piano ever so faintly. They tickle my palms.

The music rises, wraps round my shoulders, and makes me move and move, and I have no trouble following the rhythm because it's inside me. In this sea of glimmering drops, I see my submarine, the one I wanted to drive when I was little, when people would ask me what I wanted to be when I grew up.

Filippo plays it in a fun way, and I can't help but sing the chorus and sway in time on the stool, laughing. He smiles too, right through to the last note. We both take our hands off the piano.

I applaud just for him. "Well done!"

"I'll teach you if you want."

The joy of the moment vanishes instantly. "I can't read the notes."

"It doesn't matter. I played without music."

"Another time, maybe."

"Promise?"

I feel my face go red. "Only if you keep practicing your modern songs."

"Okay. It's a deal." We shake hands and I try not to squeeze too hard, scared I'll ruin his musician's fingers.

The reception is almost over, and the parents are putting on their coats to go home. Mom and Dad are talking to a young woman with very dark hair. "Mom!" Filippo runs up to her and hugs her. He's almost the same height as her.

"We were talking about you," Dad says. I hate it when grown-ups do that. They never tell you what it was they were saying.

"Can they come over to our house?" Filippo asks his mom. Her face is round and pale, like the moon, and she has big eyes.

"Of course they can. Shall we get something else to eat?"

Dad puts on his coat. "We could order pizza. What do you think, Mafalda?"

"I'd love that! I always want pizza."

"Especially pepperoni pizza," Filippo added.

"Oh yes, definitely pepperoni."

Filippo lives above a shop where they print T-shirts with personalized messages on them. His mom works there; that's why he has a jacket with his name on it. You can print whatever you like, not just T-shirts, but also cushions, tablecloths, towels, all sorts of things. It must be great to work somewhere like that! Filippo says he'll take me there one day and turn on the print-ing machines just for me.

On the drive there, his mom tells us the shop came with the apartment, but business is not good at the moment. Everyone just orders everything online. "When I'm grown up, I'll become a coder so I can make you a website and print T-shirts online,"

Filippo says to his mom. She strokes his cheek.

The three of us are sitting in the back of Dad's car—Filippo is in the middle, and we're squashed against the windows.

"Or I'll buy you a perfume shop," he continues. "It's what you've always dreamed of!"

"Really, Christine?" Mom says, turning round to look at us in the back. "In fact, the perfume you're wearing now is really nice."

She's right. It smells of hazelnut and caramel. Delicious.

"Oh, thank you. I made it myself. I'll show you when we get home."

The apartment is on the second floor. It's just Filippo and his mom, Christine, who live there. They don't even have a cat. Filippo whispers to me that his mom talks to the plants, especially the geraniums on the balcony. "They're my other babies!" she sings.

I get the impression Mom likes Christine and her plant-talking, because she's laughing a lot and I haven't seen her laugh this much in ages. She helps Filippo's mom set the table. Dad calls the pizza restaurant to order, and while we're waiting, Filippo shows me his room. It's small and there are action figures everywhere. I know because I step on one as soon as I go in. I pick it up and look for somewhere to put it. I notice the shelves are all full. "Wow, nice."

"My dad buys me them every now and then. I hate them."

"You can't say you hate the things you have."

Filippo throws himself on the bed, kicks off his shoes, and turns on a mini television set sitting on a tiny shelf. "But you told me you hate Christmas."

"That's right. You remember everything, don't you?"

"Not really. The opposite, to be honest. For the past few months, I've tried not to remember anything. Come over here."

I take my shoes off and sit down beside him. Piano music is playing on the television. I recognize it—it's the song Filippo played earlier, the yellow submarine one. "Let's sing," he says, and starts jumping on the bed. I feel like giggling, and even though I can't read the song lyrics on the screen, I sing the words I remember and jump on the bed too.

"We yall live in a lellow subraminnnnne. . . ."

We sing louder and louder, holding a shoe up as a microphone. My glasses fall off, but we keep going till the music stops. Then we dive off the edge of the bed, falling to the floor where we lie to catch our breath.

Filippo twists around after a bit to look at me. His face is close to mine, but without my glasses, it could be miles away. A huge gray cloud is obscuring most of it, and I wonder if he can see it in my eyes.

"What color are my eyes?" I ask him.

"Brown. Why?"

"Can you see anything in them?"

He waits for a few seconds. I think he's staring at my pupils. "No, nothing. Just . . ."

There, I knew it. He can see signs of the mist.

"Just lots of green and yellow streaks. Like a forest full of mushrooms."

It's not great as compliments go, but I like forests. Better than Stargardt mist, for sure.

"Why, what did you think was there?"

I look down at my socks, or rather, where I think my socks are. "It doesn't matter. Sometimes I think people can see my mist."

"Your mist? What do you mean?"

Filippo seems genuinely interested. He's sitting cross-legged in front of me, practically staring at me, his nose just a centimeter from mine.

"Stop it." I push him away, and he starts laughing, then comes straight back up close. I snort. "I'll tell you if you promise not to laugh."

"It's a deal."

"There are spots in my eyes that are getting bigger and bigger. . . ."

"Lots of them?"

"No. Just two. One in one eye and one in the other."

"Are they there all the time?"

"They weren't at the beginning. Now they're quite big, and I see them all the time. They blot things out and get darker when I'm tired."

"I get it. And can't you get rid of them?"

"No."

"What about the mist?"

"It comes with the spots, and it makes everything look hazy, not just where the spots are."

"That's not good. Are you scared?"

When I don't reply, Filippo pulls himself up from the floor and asks me if I've ever studied music before.

"No, why?

"You sing well."

"Don't be silly."

"No, really. You never miss a note. Come here."

He fishes something out of the wardrobe. A guitar. He takes off the cover and sits on the bed with it, plucking the strings.

"Do you play guitar?"

He doesn't reply. But plays a note. "This is 'Do.' Copy me."

"This is 'Do.'"

"No!" Filippo laughs. "Copy the note. With your voice. Sing 'Do.' Like this." He plucks the strings and sings. *"Dooo . . ."*

I do it too, even though I'm embarrassed.

"See? You're good. Now this is 'Re.' *Reeee . . .*"

I copy him.

"It comes so naturally to you. You're lucky."

I find it impossible not to smile. It's not often I feel lucky about something I don't need eyes for. Or glasses.

Dad pops his head round the door to call us for dinner; the pizza's here. Filippo races into the hall and I follow, trying to overtake him. We push and shove, both wanting to get into the kitchen first.

When we sit down, Mom pushes my pigtails behind my shoulders. "Where are your glasses, Mafalda?"

I'm about to admit I dropped them and didn't bother looking for them. In fact, I completely forgot about them, but Filippo replies for me. "We were singing. She didn't need them."

Dad puts a slice of pizza on my plate. "We'll look for them later, okay? Don't leave them behind."

No one seems angry. To make a good impression on Filippo's mom, I lay my napkin on my knee and start cutting my pizza with a knife and fork.

"Do you want a black olive?" Filippo asks. "I don't like them, but one's ended up on my plate by mistake."

I don't have to worry about finding it without my glasses. Filippo pops it straight into my mouth. He probably doesn't have the best manners, but he certainly solves a lot of problems. I think back to the bit in *The Baron in the Trees* where Cosimo is in the tree with the Spanish girl and everything seems wonderful and easy, not like with the other girl, Viola, who used to drive him mad. Maybe that's the difference between friendship and love. Being friends is easy; being in love gets your head all in a muddle, a bit like the Stargardt mist in my eyes.

After the pizza, our moms put on their jackets and go down to Emanuela's bakery to buy some pastries. Dad stays to look after us but actually just sits on the sofa, which is in the kitchen, and watches something funny on television.

Filippo wants to go onto the balcony to show me the dried-up geraniums his mom talks to, but Dad stops us. "Jackets," he says.

I pick up my down jacket and Filippo pulls on his usual blue one with his name on the back. Dad stops him again. "Have you not got a warmer one, son? It's freezing outside."

Filippo says nothing. It's my turn to reply for him.

"Dad, do you know it was Filippo's birthday not so long ago?"

"Really? Happy belated birthday, Filippo."

"Right. And I didn't give him a present because he didn't have a party."

Filippo kicks my leg in a what-are-you-doing kind of way.

"Do you remember that spare jacket you keep in the trunk of the car for when you have to make deliveries up in the mountains? The one you don't like anymore."

Come on, Dad, work it out. You must know where I'm going with this.

"The green and purple one?"

"Yes, that one. Maybe it would fit Filippo."

Dad thinks for a few seconds, then exclaims, "Of course it would make an excellent birthday present! You know, it's not that I don't like it, Filippo; it's just that I hardly ever use it and I've been wanting to give it to someone for a while." Dad picks up the car keys and goes to the door of the apartment. "I was thinking of giving it to my nephew, but you beat him to it. I'll go and get it." The door closes behind him.

I wonder if Filippo will be annoyed with me. He squeezes my wrist tight and pulls me into a room that I think is the bathroom. It's very white and smells of lemon. I hear him rummage around before he places a glass bottle in my hand.

"What is it?"

"Smell it."

I bring the bottle up to my nose. It has the scent of those little blue flowers Grandma used to call "Mary's eyes." The garden outside our building is always full of them. My eyes start to nip. I have to blink a few times. I'm sure it must be the perfume.

"Nice. Did your mom make it?"

"Yes. You can have it. In exchange for the jacket."

I stand and inhale the lovely smell. My eyes are used to it now. "Won't your mom be angry?"

"Who cares. She makes loads every month. She'll never notice."

"Okay. Thanks. Listen . . ." I have to ask him. "You want to be my friend, don't you?"

"What if I do?" he says, shutting the perfume drawer.

"Why do you want us to be friends?"

Filippo leaps forward and sprays me with the perfume I'm holding. Then he runs into his bedroom, shouting, "Because we can form a band when we're big! I'll play the instruments and you can sing!" I follow him, laughing, and think it sounds like a great idea.

* * *

I'm in bed with Ottimo Turcaret at my feet. He won't let me pet him tonight because he can smell my new perfume, which wouldn't wash off, not even in the shower. I borrowed Dad's phone to look up how to become a singer. There are apparently at least fifteen stages to go through, but I couldn't work out where you do them.

It also says on the phone that you need something special, something no one else has. I don't know if I like Filippo's idea of a band so much now. The only special things I have are a brown-and-gray cat (I don't think there are many others like him) and mist in my eyes. I'm the opposite kind of special. I blink and throw my personal organizer on the floor. I kneel down to flick through it, almost ripping the pages, then hastily scribble something, pressing far too hard on the pen.

Eat black olives because I can't see what color they really are.

Sing in a band.

I climb into bed and pull the covers up over my head. Darkness is not a room with no doors or windows. Darkness is a monster that eats your black olives and your dreams.

> *Cosimo, it's snowing, and I've just realized I could freeze to death in winter in the school cherry tree.*

But then I remembered that you survived, and when it was time to die, you grabbed on to a passing hot-air balloon and let yourself fall into the sea, so you would never ever touch land. I can't really hunt furry animals to make myself blankets, like you did, so I'll have to work out what to do if I feel like I'm freezing to death. Will you help me think of something?

PS: Say thanks to Grandma for the blanket. I'll take it to the tree.

14

Making Good-Night Light Signals Out the Window, Counting the Stars in the Sky at Night

My special-needs teacher is called Fernando. He's young and very boring.

He spends all his time with his nose in books written in Chinese, which you read back to front, and messaging on his phone. What he should be doing is checking that I write things correctly in my notebook, that I don't get lost going around school, and that I do the braille exercises. Luckily, he doesn't seem too bothered about these things, and most of the time he leaves me alone. He only switches on, like a robot, when another teacher goes by and he pretends to be helping me write.

He'll be on the school ski trip, but he'll be too busy looking after Oscar, who's in a wheelchair, to be worrying about me. It sometimes feels like no one knows about my Stargardt mist, although I know they know. Maybe they forget because you can't see it—my mist, that is. My eyes look normal from the outside. It's a bit like being crazy. A crazy person looks normal on the outside, but then they start screaming and everyone remembers. The gym teacher once said, "Poor girl, she can't see," talking about me, and I wanted to scream so she'd think *I* was crazy and leave me alone.

Mom and Dad knock on the window of the bus where I'm sitting (front row, beside Fernando) and wave goodbye, as if I were going away on a long journey. I mouth *bye* and quickly look the other way. The other parents aren't standing as close to the bus, and everyone onboard is already busy with their tablets, their earbuds, or playing with their phones and don't bother waving. Filippo, wearing the jacket Dad gave him, is the only one who can't sit still. He's in the back and keeps playing jokes on his friends. I hear them screaming, "Stop putting my hood up! I want to sleep!"

Sleeping is impossible because as soon as we set off, the teacher pulls out the bus microphone and starts explaining the schedule for the next two days. Tonight, the girls will sleep in one chalet and the boys in another.

Tomorrow, we'll be visiting an organic farm and then going to the slopes in the afternoon. Those who know how to ski can go with Fernando and the gym teacher who said poor me, and the others can go sledding. I learned how to ski when I was seven. My cousin Andrea taught me, but Mom and Dad were too scared to let me go down a run because I wouldn't be able to see the bumps and would fall. Which means I'll go sledding, although I haven't been since I got my new glasses.

We've been traveling for an hour and a half, and it's now chaos on the bus. Filippo and his friends are singing dirty songs and ignoring the teachers trying to make them stop. It kind of makes me want to laugh. I've never heard songs like that before. We're on the hairpin bends now, and I hear Roly behind me starting to feel sick. He's always sick on school trips because of his motion sickness. Plus, in the time we've been on the bus, I've heard him rip open at least three granola bars and pop two cans of Fanta, so that can't be helping.

Since Roly's sitting right behind us, I tell Fernando, and he twists round to have a look. Right away he yells at the driver to stop.

I feel a paper ball hit my head and I jerk round. Filippo is making his way down the aisle, scoffing at poor Roly.

I glare at him. "Don't you know it's wrong to mock someone who's not well?"

"But he was eating like a pig!"

"And? He's not well now; you shouldn't laugh. Would you like people to do the same to you?"

Filippo sits down in Fernando's seat while he's out in the street with Roly. Then he kneels against the backrest and tells everyone to be quiet. "That's enough now. The next person I hear laughing will get thumped when we get off." No one speaks, except for one of the teachers who tells him to go back to his seat.

Filippo leans over me and says quickly, under his breath, "When they let you choose your bed tonight, pick one by the window."

"Why?"

"Just do it. Can you stay awake until midnight?"

"Of course I can."

"Well, look out at midnight. I'll say good night from our chalet."

"How will you do that?"

"You'll see me."

"But I—"

"Don't worry, you'll see me. But don't tell anyone."

He scoots off to the back of the bus just as Fernando comes back to sit beside me.

* * *

We've been at the chalet for two hours. We had soup and hot sandwiches for dinner, and now we've got to put our stuff away before going to bed.

It's good that I have to stay awake until midnight as it gives me time to study everyone else's bags and see if there's anything useful for when I move into the cherry tree. Maybe I'll be able to get something tonight. I took the bed by the window—it's drafty, but it doesn't matter. I can see outside from here, and I can keep an eye on all the other girls' beds and sleeping bags.

Chiara is blowing up her air mattress. She's going to sleep on it with Martina. The teachers said it was okay. The girls in my class are crowded around her, and I know they'd all like to sleep on it too, or at least try it. If we'd still been good friends, Chiara would've picked me. But it's not essential, like Estella says. If I've understood it properly, a thing is essential only if you need it to live, and I can live without Chiara's mattress. Of course, it would be nice to have it in the cherry tree.

I won't be able to take it tonight, though. They'll be sleeping on it, obviously. I'll have to wait until tomorrow when we pack everything up to leave and go down for breakfast. Maybe I'll pretend to be sick and go back to the dormitory. If Fernando lets me go on my own, I'd be free to take the mattress. I've left a compartment in my duffel bag empty, the one with the zipper that's tucked under all my clothes, so I'd have somewhere to put it. Once I blow it up and lay it across the branches, it will be really comfortable.

We've got to put on our pajamas. The teachers stay with us until we're all in bed, then they turn out the lights and warn us that they'll be back in an hour because they have some paperwork to finish for our visit tomorrow. The girls in my class and the ones from sixth grade wait for the sound of the teachers' steps to disappear. Even though I can still hear the teachers going down the stairs, the girls jump out of bed and start chatting. One of the oldest gets up and goes to turn on a light.

I pull myself up too. Chiara and Martina are lying on their stomachs, listening to songs on Martina's iPod, sharing the earphones. I know this because they're moving their heads in rhythm and singing quietly, out of tune. The hand of Francesca, my friend from Sicily, reaches out to me from a bunk bed, holding an open packet of gummy bears. I take a couple and stick them in my mouth. "Fanks."

I wouldn't mind listening to some music too. I'm still rummaging around in my duffel under the bed when the girl who switched on the light walks over to me and sits down on my duvet. "Hi, you're Mafalda, aren't you?"

I scrunch up at the pillow end of the bed and hug my knees. "Yes, why?"

"No reason."

She's tall, has messy brown hair with reddish glints, and is wearing pajamas that are not really pajamas, just a top with writing on it and a pair of blue leggings. Two of her friends follow her over and sit down, one beside her and one on the floor. They smile at me. "So, is this the famous Mafalda?"

"Yes." The first one smiles.

I don't understand. "Why famous?"

The girls glance at one another, still smiling. "We shouldn't really tell you. . . ."

"But we can't resist!"

"Who's going to tell her?"

"I will!"

"No, I will!"

"If you ask me, Emilia should tell her," the one on the floor finally says.

I ask who Emilia is.

The first girl points at herself. "I'm Emilia, Filippo's ex. Pleased to meet you."

I suddenly feel flustered and my face goes red. My glasses steam up too, so it takes me a while to read the writing on her top—it's her name, Emilia. It looks similar to the writing on Filippo's blue jacket.

The girls laugh. Luckily, the ones from my class are doing their own thing. "I'm Mafalda" is all I manage to say. But they knew that already.

Too late. "We know that!" cackles the other girl sitting on the bed. I think she lives near my house. Her name's Julie, I remember.

"Yes, we know, we know," Emilia says. "Filippo's school diary has your name all over it. Mafalda here, Mafalda there . . . There's even a heart beside your birthday."

"That's not true."

"It is. Your birthday's on the first of February, isn't it?"

Oh dear. A heart?

"Don't worry, I'm not jealous." Emilia pats me on the back. "We broke up, or I should say, I broke up with him. In October. His dad started his disappearing act again, and Filippo didn't take it too well. He went really crazy, so I ditched him."

"Oh." I don't know what to say.

"So, do you like him?"

The three girls huddle around me. I'd like the ground to open up and swallow me, I'm so embarrassed. "Who, Filippo? No, we're just friends!"

The other two start jumping around and clapping their hands. "I think she likes him!"

Emilia takes my hand. "Mafalda, haven't you seen how he behaves? He's a hooligan; he's always shouting. He might even fail the year."

I look down at my socks. "I've heard rumors that he's a bit crazy. . . ."

"A bit crazy? He's been *wild* since his parents divorced! If you two get together, you'd better be careful!"

So, it's true, his parents are divorced. My third eye was right this time too.

"But I don't want to get together. I don't even know what getting together would mean."

"That you kiss," Julie says.

"And you'll get married and have children when you grow up," the other girl says.

Francesca, who's been listening from her bunk bed, pops her head out and says, "We can't have babies at our age."

"Yes we can!" Emilia says a little too loudly.

Curious now, a few of the other girls look up from their phones and tablets to hear what's being said. Emilia continues, "If a boy gets very, very close to you, a sore tummy comes, even at our age, then you throw up, and the baby grows in your sore tummy and comes out nine months later."

"From where?" Chiara asks.

"From your belly button. The doctors make a hole in it and pull the baby out. What else do you think it's for?"

Everyone squeals, disgusted.

A teacher comes in. She heard us shouting downstairs and has come to tell us to go straight to sleep. Enough talking for one night.

We get back into our beds. To make sure we stay there, the teacher decides to go to bed as well and heads into the bathroom with her things to get changed. The lights go off. Before I remove my glasses, I push the curtain aside to look outside. The sky is beautiful here, all black and blue and speckled with white dots. I haven't seen the stars for such a long time. Maybe I can see them here because we're higher up. If I can, that means I'll also be able to see them from the cherry tree. I hope so.

Otherwise, this could be the last time I see the stars.

I check my watch. It was Grandma's, but my parents gave it to me when she went to live in the tree. I bring it up close and press the light button to see what time it is—it's a quarter to midnight. The other teachers also came back and are asleep in our dormitory. One is lying on a blow-up bed near the door, snoring through her nose. It's funny. The girls in my class and the older girls are as still as can be in their beds.

Everything is steeped in dark blue, and even though I'm in a room with loads of other people, I feel like the only girl in the world.

I push the curtain aside. It was snowing when we arrived. It's not now. The fields around the chalets and the surrounding hills are light blue (that's what snow looks like at night), and the moon is like a great big streetlight, illuminating everything, although there's not much to illuminate here. Only the other small lodge where the boys are sleeping. And a light in the window. A light that comes and goes. Like a signal. Like the good-night signals I used to send to Grandma before I went to bed.

I spring to attention and whack my glasses up my nose. The light goes on and off for a bit, and then I don't see it anymore. I have to reply. When someone says good night, you have to say it back; it would be bad manners not to. But I need something to reply with, a flashlight, something that lights up. Oh, but I do have something—Grandma's watch! I take it off my wrist, put it up to the window, and press the button repeatedly. I hope he can see it from the boys' dormitory. The light from before comes back on again, flashing like mad. He saw it!

We keep signaling each other until the snoring teacher scares me when she groans in her sleep and rolls over on the mattress. I do one last signal, a long, long one, which means we have to sleep now, then wait for a reply. It comes right away, just as long. I lie back down on the bed with lots of stars in my eyes. All things considered, I feel happy. I'm not sure I know why, but I no longer feel alone in the world.

Filippo waved at me from his table this morning at breakfast, then went straight back to splashing milk at his friends.

"I told you he likes you," Emilia said as she passed behind me.

"We only said hello, and he hardly looked at me."

"That's what boys do. It's a sign. You need to get used to the signs."

The visit to the organic farm was so boring that not even Filippo could come up with a joke to distract us, or a reason to interrupt. The only nice thing was that they let us taste fresh butter and we ate so many rolls and jam, we were fit to burst. Just as well, they're taking us to the slopes next! A big group goes away with Fernando the teacher, including Emilia in her red ski suit, and Chiara, who shows everyone her ski goggles, even me, before she gets on the lift.

I go up to the top of the sledding hill, sit on the ground, and write in the snow. I can't whiz down with the others because I'm scared I'd bang into a tree. We've been given sleds that look like little cars and no one wants to share theirs with me, although I'm not sure I'd want to anyway. To go on a sled and not see anything would be weird.

A teacher comes over and asks me to go down with her. I reply that I'd rather stay where I am. She goes back to chat with the other teachers while my class-mates go up and down the hill, screaming their heads off. I'm wondering when would be the right time to pretend I don't feel well and go back to the lodge to get the things I need. A snowball hits my back, and I look round to see who threw it. Some person, scream-ing louder than everyone else, is running toward me, dragging a bright red sled behind him. I shouldn't be surprised when I realize it's Filippo. His thin glasses are spattered with snowflakes, and his smile is so big, it's almost too big for his face.

He throws himself down beside me and, right away, wants to know why I'm not joining in.

"I don't feel like it."

"That's not true. It's because you can't see, and you're scared."

What he says is true, but I stick a handful of snow down his back anyway. He screams and laughs and rolls around. I can't help but laugh too. He stops suddenly and tweaks the pink-and-gray pom-pom on my hat. Three of our classmates arrive at the top of the hill and arrange themselves along a pretend starting line to have a race. The teacher shouts "Go!" from the side of the hill and off they slide, crunching over the icy snow.

"Do you want to come down with me? You can sit behind me."

I'm not sure. Better not risk it. "No. I've seen you; you go too fast."

Filippo stands up and positions the sledge at the top of the hill. He turns to me with his hands on his hips. I think that's what he was doing the first time I saw him. "I had to promise to do something difficult."

The piano. Modern songs.

"Yes, you're right. And?"

"It's your turn now. You have to do something difficult."

I wanted to pretend I wasn't feeling well, but now I really do have an upset stomach. I try to put him off. "Who said?"

"Me!" Filippo grabs my hat by the pom-pom and whips it off my head, then climbs onto the front of the sled. Resigned, I go over to him. Another two people from our class have arrived with their sleds. "Want to race?" Filippo asks them. They accept right away and get into position on our left. "Get on! Jeez, what are you waiting for?"

I get in behind Filippo and only just manage to get my hat back before it flies away as we take off down the hill at breakneck speed. I grip on to his back and scream in his ear that he's going too fast.

He turns his head slightly in my direction. "You want me to go slow in a race?"

"I know, but I can't see anything!"

"Neither can I!" He turns all the way round to show me his goggles covered in snow. Panic-stricken, I yelp.

"We're going to crash!"

"Maybe!" He guffaws, laughing like someone whose parents are not divorced and who is simply having a ball in the snow. "Shut your eyes! It's awesome! I'll brake if we go offtrack!"

The hill's not that long. On either side of us there are only sprinklings of snow and the green and brown of the woods along the edge of the ski run. We're winning the race. I can't hear the other sleds, so I do what Filippo says—I shut my eyes. I feel the cold wind of the descent on my face, my hair flying in the wind and my heart pounding. Or is it Filippo's? I can feel it in his back. What does it matter? Hurtling down like this, the screams of the others so far away in the distance, only the noise of the sled under me, is truly wonderful. And weird. Like walking with a scarf over your eyes, only more dizzying. I'm absolutely petrified. Yet I want this descent to last an hour, a day, forever.

The screams of the others cheering at the finish line are growing louder, and the hill stops being a hill. Applause rings loud in our ears as we blast into a mound of fresh snow. Snowflakes swirl gently around us, and we laugh and laugh; we laugh so hard we can hardly breathe, then we get up and dance around in a circle, shrieking, "We won!"

When our opponents finish, I feel a strange fluttering in my tummy, and I think I'm going to be sick. "What's wrong? Don't you feel well?" Filippo asks. I don't answer. I go over to a bush and do what Roly did yesterday.

Fernando takes me to the lodge we slept in.

The lady from the hotel makes me a cup of tea. It will calm my stomach, she says, and then we go upstairs. Fernando lets me go in by myself to go to the bathroom. "I'll wait for you in the lobby," he tells me, pulling one of his Chinese language books out of his jacket. This is it. I go into the dormitory. All the beds have been made, and the backpacks of their occupants stand beside them. I see a fuzzy red-and-blue ball in the corner—it's Chiara's mattress. Hands trembling slightly, I pick it up and stuff it into my duffel bag, hiding it as best I can. There's nothing else I need from here. For a second, I think a tablet might be useful for my life in the tree, but then I remember I'll be in the dark. What's more, it's too expensive to steal. I couldn't do that.

I go downstairs, duffel over my shoulder. We're leaving soon, so it makes sense. Fernando is sitting in a red armchair, absorbed in his book. I have to find a way of getting into the boys' lodge now. The lady who made me tea earlier speaks to me as I walk past the desk. "How are you feeling?"

"So-so," I reply, which is not a lie.

"I've got a present for you, since you've not been feeling well."

She leans over the counter and places an odd-looking gray flower in my hand.

"What is it?"

"Edelweiss."

I touch the flower gently—it looks like it might turn to dust any minute.

"It's all hairy!"

"Yes. Have you never seen one before?"

"No, but it's beautiful. Thank you."

Fernando comes over to see the Edelweiss as well. "Interesting," he pronounces.

I have an idea.

"Fernando, would you help me with something?"

He takes me to the door of the lodge. "Hmmm, what is it?"

I pull him by the jacket and point to the boys' chalet. "I'd really like to surprise a boy in the other class."

"A boy?"

"Yes. A boy I like."

"Ah."

"Could you take me into their dorm so I can put the edelweiss on his pillow?"

Fernando gives a little snort. "All right, but be quick about it."

The boys' dorm smells disgusting.

Fernando stands on guard outside in the corridor, so I have to be quick. I wander around until I find Roly's pink lunch box and slip it straight into my bag. There's no sign of Christian's waterproof jacket anywhere. Maybe he took it out with him this morning.

Fernando sticks his head round the door. "Finished?"

He scared me. Just as well, I'd already hidden the lunchbox. I go over to a bed that's right under the window, with a view straight across to the girls' lodge. There's a torch on it. I place the edelweiss on the pillow and leave.

"Sorry, Fernando. I couldn't find the right bed."

"It's okay. You don't want to get the wrong person with stuff like this. Let's go and wait on the bus."

Mom's emptying my duffel from the trip. I can see a faint flicker of light coming from the bathroom.

I'm in bed, but I'm not worried because I've already taken the pink lunch box and the mattress out of my bag and hidden them under my clothes in the wardrobe. I can keep the light on for another ten minutes, Mom and Dad said. But I don't have much to do. I lift my personal organizer and black pen from the shelf and cross out *Counting the stars in the sky at night.*

I know, Cosimo. I took my classmates' things without telling them. I shouldn't have done that. But you helped the brigands too, remember? You knew they weren't bad; they just had to behave a bit badly to get enough food to eat. Please don't tell Grandma.

I promise that when I'm grown-up in the cherry tree and have learned to build things the way you did, I'll give everything back. It'll take time, but one day I will.

Loving Someone

I'm going to have a baby.

I'm almost certain now.

Since we got back from the ski trip, I haven't been able to stop thinking about what Emilia said about how having a baby means you get a sore tummy and then you're sick. I think about it all the time—while I'm rubbing Ottimo Turcaret behind the ears, before and after my homework, even now as I walk to school.

You get a sore tummy then you're sick. That's what happened to me when we were sledding. I don't know if you need a boy as well, but I did hug Filippo really tight when we were in the race. That must be it. What will I say to Mom? Will Ottimo Turcaret still love me? I'll have to leave school, and how will I look after a baby in the darkness?

I imagined having six children when I was little—five girls and a boy—then I got the mist in my eyes and I stopped thinking about it. I'd lose them in the mist, or I'd comb their hair silly, or they'd starve because I can't drive to the supermarket to do the shopping. Maybe I could order pizza for dinner, but that's not healthy. No, I can't have children. Just Ottimo Turcaret. He sorts his food out himself, and he cleans his coat and keeps it tidy.

I have to tell someone. Estella. She's the only one who can help me. I'll go to her room when the bell rings for break. To stop thinking about it, I count how many steps it takes me to get to the cherry tree, all brown and skinny, from when I can see it. One, two, three . . .

Eighty steps, maybe seventy-eight.

Forty meters, maybe thirty-nine.

Another ten steps and I hear it—Estella's whistle. If I lose my hearing as well, I really will be in trouble.

I knock two or three times on the door of the janitors' room. It's lunch, and everyone is running up and down the corridors, clutching half-open snack bars in their hands. Three boys from Filippo's class are playing basketball with the wastepaper basket, using scrunched-up tinfoil as a ball. I'd like to play too, but I've got more important things on my mind. Estella opens the door and I go inside, leaving some of the chaos, not all of it, behind me.

Estella throws me a bag of chips.

"Are you not having any?" I say.

She flops, or kind of collapses, onto the swivel chair. She props her head up on her hand, elbow on the table. She looks tired. Her face is the color of lemons when they go moldy, which is actually a beautiful color, only it doesn't seem nice to tell someone that.

Estella gestures that she doesn't want any chips and pulls a stool closer to her chair. I like being here because everything is nearby and I can see things. I sit on the stool. It's time to tell her I'm going to be a mom.

I make a little noise with the chip bag I'm holding and, without looking anywhere in particular, launch into my speech. "Estella, do you have a child?"

She raises her head and spins the chair round to face me. She really does look tired. "No. I've never had one."

"Why?"

"Why do you want to know?"

I fill my mouth with chips to hide my embarrass-ment. "Well, because children interest me."

Estella's eyes open so wide, even I can see every tiny detail, including the white bit around her pupils. "Children interest you? Listen to you. You're not in love, are you, Mafalda?"

I look at her from behind my glasses, not knowing what to say, and I feel like I've gone red from the top of my head to the tips of my toes. How did she work it out? Even I hadn't known, until now.

Estella laughs—not a mocking laugh, I under-stand that. My third eye tells me it's a kind laugh, for something good, like good luck.

"Oh, Mafalda, some good news at last! I'm delighted to hear that. Now I can die happy."

"Why is it good news? How can you say that?"

She brings her chair up close so she's sitting right in front of me and takes hold of my shoulders. Her nose is as thin and skinny as a branch on the cherry tree, and her bright pink lipstick is slightly faded. "I just know," she says. "And it's about time it happened to you. Love is always good news, Mafalda. Never forget that. Everyone falls in love. Children and old people and people who live far away and bad people . . . they all fall in love."

"Bad people? You mean like Dracula?"

"Yes. Even Dracula had a wife. It may sound strange, but it's true. Do you know why it's so wonderful? Because it means we're all equal. In love, the poor are richer and the rich are happier."

"Is it because it's essential?"

"Yes, for many people it is."

"Is it for you?"

She lets go of my shoulders and sighs. "It was. I had a husband in Romania. But after a while, we stopped saying 'I love you.'"

"Is that why you don't have children?"

"I think so. If you don't tell the other person you love them enough, and they don't tell you, it's better not to have children."

I think I understand. The rule is if I don't tell Filippo I love him, I won't have a baby. Got it. All I have to do is say nothing. Talking to Estella is always really useful. She knows about things and she always tells me the truth. I go into the corridor and almost run to class. It's not that love makes you see better; it just makes you less afraid of bumping into things.

I'm just home from school.

I dump my backpack on the floor by the door and run into my room, or at least try to get there as quickly as possible without bumping into anything.

I get my personal organizer and turn to the second page. If I've understood it correctly, to have a baby, I have to tell its dad I love him. But I can't have children because you can't give a bottle in the darkness or change diapers and all the other things babies need. So, all I have to do is never tell anyone I love them. I pick up my black pen and cross out *Loving someone*.

Part Five

Thirty Meters

16

She'll Find Me Anyway

*H*appy birthday to youuu, happy birthday to youuu... Happy birthday, dear Mafaldaaaaaaa..."

Mom comes into the darkened living room with a cake full of candles that light up her face and her smile. You'd think she was alone in the room with a choir hiding behind the couch singing "Happy Birthday." I'm sitting at the coffee table with my legs crossed under it and my aunt, my uncle, Andrea, Ravina, Dad, and Filippo are all around me, sitting on the sofa and on the floor. Chiara couldn't come, her mom said. It's a lie, but I don't care; I only invited her because Mom and Dad insisted. They're sad we're no longer friends. Don't they know that friends come and go as you grow up? Ottimo Turcaret is hiding under the coffee table where he thinks he's safe—he's not used to the commotion. But Mom plants the cake right on top of his hiding place and he makes a run for it, and also to get away from the very loud "Happy birthday to youuuuuuu!" singing.

I puff my cheeks up like a hot-air balloon and blow so hard that some of the frosting spatters onto the carpet. I can normally blow all the candles out in a single puff, but not this year. One is still lit, and I have to breathe in again if I'm going to cast the room into complete darkness. Everyone claps their hands and shouts at me to make a wish. The smoke from the candles goes in my eyes. I shut them, thinking about my wish, but all of a sudden, I'm scared. I open my eyes very slowly, and the darkness is still there. I shut them again and count to ten while the others keep asking what I'm wishing for. I try raising just one eyelid a tiny bit. It's okay; someone has turned on the light, and I can see nearly everyone now, and the cake and the rows of balloons Dad has strung from the ceiling right out to the corners of the room. (They look like cherries on branches.) It would have been awful to have ended up in the darkness, today of all days, on my eleventh birthday.

Luckily, Mom has already started cutting the cake, so there are no more questions about my wish. Filippo comes to eat his slice beside me at the coffee table. He uses a fork, but he's wolfing it down so quickly, he still manages to get the cake over most of his face. My aunt is watching him. She looks worried and also slightly disgusted. He turns to her and points to the cake with his fork, smeared in cream and lumps of cake. "Iw wealy wood!"

My aunt looks even more concerned, but she replies, "Thank you, Filippo," because she made the cake. I grin quietly to myself, like Ottimo Turcaret when Estella hasn't seen him doing his business in the school vegetable garden.

The housephone rings. With all the racket going on, I'm the only one who hears the first ring, although it almost felt like a whisper of air had brushed my face at the same time that I heard the shrill, piercing sound. Dad eventually hears it too and goes to answer in the other room. He comes back in quickly and calls me. "Someone wants to say 'happy birthday.'"

I follow him into the kitchen and sit down at the table. Dad passes me the phone and leaves me with Mom, who's filling the dishwasher.

"Hello."

"Happy birthday, little princess."

"Who is . . . ?"

"The queen of the Amazons—don't you recognize me?"

The voice seems so very, very tiny—not the big, shouty one that yells at me to go back to the classroom or do something by myself—that I almost don't recognize her.

"Estella! Where are you?"

"I'm in the hospital."

"Doing what?"

Silence on her side. Quite a long silence. "I'm visiting a friend."

"Is she sick?"

"No, not her. Let's say she works here."

Maybe her friend who works in the hospital is Doctor Olga! I'm about to ask when she starts speaking again. "So, is your party good fun?"

"Yes, but I'm sorry you're not here."

"I'm sorry too. Parties are wonderful things. Try to have lots and lots of fun. I'll make sure you get my present tomorrow at school."

"What do you mean, make sure I get it? Won't you be there?"

"No, not tomorrow. This friend of mine is here for a while, and I have to look after her."

"Can I meet her?"

"Better not. No, better never. I will never ever ever let you meet her, Mafalda."

I'm a little jealous.

"Okay, bye, then."

"Bye. Don't forget your present. I'll put it in the janitors' room, in the chip drawer."

"Okay. Say hello to your friend."

There's a long silence. Finally, in a strange voice, she says, "Happy birthday, Mafalda, my little princess." And hangs up.

My glasses are all steamed up. A thought occurs to me—maybe it was Estella who left the note on my desk a few weeks ago?

"Are you coming to open your presents? Here, open mine first!" Filippo comes running into the kitchen and doesn't put the brakes on in time. He sends the chair, the present, and everything around him flying into me, and we end up practically inside the dishwasher. Mom climbs over us in her high heels (she wore them today, even though it's not a high-heel day), opens the fridge, takes out the fruit salad, and shuts the fridge door.

"Yes, I think you should go and open your presents in the other room, Mafalda. Filippo's dad is coming to pick him up in half an hour."

For a second, I hope that Filippo's box contains a T-shirt with my name on it, like the one he gave Emilia. What I actually find is so much better. I don't understand what it is at first. It looks like a kind of miniature stereo. There's also a microphone. A real one, not a plastic toy.

"It's a special karaoke machine," Filippo says, picking up the box and weaving his way through the guests to the television. I watch him press a few buttons, then connect the microphone cable somewhere behind the screen. He starts the program with the karaoke machine's remote control and explains. "Someone sings a song so you can listen and learn it. Then the music starts, and you can sing it on your own. If you can't remember the words, you go back and listen again."

A song I've heard a few times on the radio in Mom's car starts up on the screen. Andrea gets up from the couch and takes the microphone. "*There was this guy who, just like me, loved the Beatles and the Rolling Stones. . . .*"

For a music teacher, he's not that great a singer. The others don't seem to notice, and they join in. I go over to Filippo and, slightly shouting to make myself heard over the others but also mumbling so no one will hear me, mutter "thank you" into his ear. "I love it."

It's a pity I won't be able to use my lovely present

much, though. I wonder if I should tell Filippo about my plan to live in the cherry tree. He seems to be looking for something in the plastic bag the karaoke was in. "There's a card, too," he says, handing me a blue envelope.

I take it without saying anything. I have a quick look around—no one is taking any notice of us, so I drag Filippo out to the hall.

"I'll read it in bed tonight. Is that okay?"

He puts his hands on his hips. "Why not now?"

I turn the card over in my hands. "Because I can't read it."

"Use your magnifying glass."

My eyebrows climb so high up my forehead, they practically connect with my hair. "How do you know I have a magnifying glass?"

"I saw you put it in your pocket one day. Go on, use it now. Why bother carrying it around if you don't use it?"

"I'm embarrassed. I never use it in front of anyone." Filippo doesn't move and says nothing. I give up.

"Okay. But let's go into my room."

We sneak along the hall to my bedroom. Ottimo Turcaret is on the bed and only lets out a solitary meow when Filippo pulls him by his front legs to put him on his knee. I sit beside them and open the envelope.

Inside is a sheet of paper folded in half, with big black marks on it.

"I used a jumbo marker pen," he announces proudly.

I take my Sherlock Holmes magnifying glass out of my pocket. I bring it up to one eye and put the paper on the other side.

> *Many happy returns on your birthday!*
> *Kisses from*
> *Filippo, Christine, and Mauro*

"Is Mauro your dad?"

"Yes."

We sit quietly on the bed for a while. Ottimo Turcaret lets Filippo rub him behind his ears and I watch, although I can't actually see much. I think about the names on the card.

"Are you with him this week?"

It's the first time we've talked about it.

"Just yesterday and today—the weekend."

"Aren't you happy to see him?"

Filippo shrugs and keeps patting Ottimo Turcaret. "No. It's his fault I went a bit crazy."

"Who says?"

"The psychologists. Even the one at school. She says I've been having trouble concentrating and I get angry too quickly since my parents divorced."

"But you don't do it on purpose." It looks like Filippo's clear glasses have steamed up, so I put an arm round him. He doesn't move, just starts crying, sobs racking his whole body; his back, his legs, even his feet are shaking. Ottimo Turcaret jumps off Filippo's knees because of the shaking and repositions himself on my desk chair. The only thing Filippo doesn't cry with is his voice. We sit in silence in my bedroom until the grown-ups call us, ruining everything as usual, even crying that makes no noise.

"Mafalda, turn out the light."

I'm lying on the bed in my pajamas; Ottimo Turcaret's on my tummy. My eyes are shut, for once. I don't usually shut my eyes, except when I'm walking in the garden with the blindfold on. I'd rather keep them as wide open as the sky, so I can let in enough light to last for the rest of my life.

Earlier, after everyone had gone home from the party, Dad took down the lines of balloons from the ceiling and I asked him if I could keep one. I put it under the bed because it'll come in handy as a hot-air balloon to fly away from the cherry tree if I can't stay there any longer, maybe because of the cold or when I'm getting old.

So I have to rest my eyes tonight. I'm not tired, honest, but my eyes are. I reach behind me to my lamp, to where I know the switch to turn it off should be. Mom comes into my room, so I open my eyelids a tiny bit to see what a mom looks like in the dark. The mint-ice-pop smell reaches me first. Then I see her shadow, with long hair but no face, wearing black clothes full of the night, which is a bit darker than my bedroom with the light off. It's weird. I thought everything would just be black in the dark, but moms can make themselves seen even in the darkest dark. Maybe they can even *see* in the dark, like cats. To find their children when they're in danger. If this is true, then maybe I can be a mom too. I push myself up with my elbows. "Mom, can you find me in the dark?"

Mom sits down beside me and strokes my hair. "I can't see you in the dark, Mafalda, but I'm sure I could still find you. Time for lights-out, though; it's really late."

Mom bends over and gives me a good-night kiss. Her hair swashes against my pillow, springing back like cotton candy, only brown, not pink. I run my fingers through it until she leaves. It's so soft.

I didn't tell Mom that the dark I was referring to was mine. But she'll find me anyway.

* * *

I don't want to talk to you or Grandma tonight, Cosimo.

The two of you have everything sorted there. You use ropes to go from branch to branch, you read books, and I'm sure you haven't noticed there are only sixty steps to the cherry tree now. Did you hear that, Cosimo? Thirty meters. That's not a lot.

Your brother once talked to a wise old Frenchman about you, and he explained that you lived in the trees because, to see the earth, you have to be at the right height, or so you believed. How close do I have to be to get a good view of my tree?

17

Having a Paper-Ball-in-the-Basket Competition

Doctor Olga has green eyes, I remember.

I try to check if I'm right, but the gray cloud in front of her face is not budging. That's why I'm still here, with Mom and Dad on either side of me, on the same uncomfortable chairs as the last time.

Doctor Olga places a long, smooth wooden stick in my hand. It's a pencil.

I run my fingers up to the top and feel the usual dinosaur eraser.

"I couldn't find one with Egyptians, sorry."

It doesn't matter. I don't really like erasers. They're

not essential. To be polite, I say thank you anyway and keep the pencil in my hand as if I'm pleased with it. Doctor Olga has a spotless white notepad on her desk, and I know she lets children draw on it. It's right in front of me, so I start doodling and pretend I'm not listening while the grown-ups speak. There are so many things you need to pretend to do when you're a kid, like pretend that the light's on, that you're not crying, that you're not listening. When I'm grown up, I'll have to pretend I'm not talking about someone who is actually right beside me, like Mom and Dad are doing now.

"How's she doing, Doctor?" Dad asks.

"Not too bad."

Another thing you have to do when you're grown up is say everything the wrong way round, starting all your sentences with "not." If you ask me, "not too bad" means very bad indeed. It's like when the teacher goes to the hairdresser's, then comes back to school and asks us if we like her hair. I'm sure all the boys want to say it looks awful, but they say "not bad, miss" to please her and make her not give us a test.

Doctor Olga keeps talking. "Have you started studying braille?"

Dad says yes, that I'm practicing. "More than a little."

Another sentence that means the opposite. The only

thing I've read in braille dots is *The Little Prince*. It was beautiful, though.

Mom's voice has tears in it. "Doctor, isn't there some kind of technology that could make things easier for her?"

"There are glasses with a camera that projects images of the outside world onto undamaged areas of the eye."

More glasses? I hope not. They sound quite complicated, and if you ask me, they'd hurt, too.

"But the way things stand, they wouldn't be of any benefit. It would be better not to make her work any harder than she already is."

That was a close shave. No doubt the glasses she was talking about are ugly, and I bet they would've put the camera on my head. I would have been a laughing-stock at school.

After a few moments' silence, the doctor makes me almost jump out of my chair when she says, "What a lovely drawing, Mafalda! It looks like Van Gogh's *Starry Night*!"

I look at the sheet of paper and I'm pretty sure I only drew circles, lots and lots of gray circles. This Van Gogh man must have the mist too, if he draws like me.

* * *

The visit to see Doctor Olga wasn't a total waste, though, because I now know what to do with the dinosaur pencil she gave me yesterday.

There's complete silence in the classroom. We're doing a geometry test, and it's a hard one. I did it with the plastic shapes you can touch. Fernando the special-needs teacher gave me a score of check minus, and now he's reading his Chinese book at an empty desk at the back of the classroom. He nearly always gives me check minus. Check for hard work and the minus because a perfect score would be too much, he explains.

I turn round slowly. Kevin is poring over lines of symmetry. He finds it really difficult.

"Psst."

He looks up from the test but then straight back down again.

I need the teacher to go and get a coffee. Since I've finished my test, I offer to get one from the machine for her, hoping it will make her start to want one. "Miss," I say quietly, leaning over her desk, "can I go and get you a coffee today?"

She shoves her phone hastily into her bag—I know she's been playing games because her phone dings quietly at every point, and I'm the only one who hears it—and says no. "I'll go. You keep a note of anyone who talks."

She lays a sheet of paper on the desk, picks up her bag, and goes out. Good. I can try again now. Kevin is tapping his black-and-yellow pencil on the edge of his desk, which he's hanging over side of. He just doesn't get lines of symmetry. I try to bring Fernando into focus, at the back, near the cupboard. I don't want him to see what I'm up to. He looks quite relaxed. I rest an elbow on Kevin's desk and whisper, "Hey, do you want a dinosaur?"

I know he likes stuff like that. Snakes, reptiles, anything green and dinosaur-like. Unsurprisingly, he bolts upright from being flopped forward and says yes right away.

"Let's swap, then." I put a hand over my mouth. "See this pencil?"

I pull the pencil with the dinosaur eraser out of my pocket.

"Cool!" Kevin says.

"Shhh," Fernando says, without taking his nose out of his book.

I lay my pencil out for Kevin to inspect. "It's yours if you bring me something."

"What?"

"I really like your waterproof jacket, the poncho one that you bring on school trips. Want to swap it?"

Kevin doesn't waste any time thinking about it.

"Not a chance. I can get a pencil like that in the shops."

It didn't work. My glasses steam up. "You can't get these in the shops. No one else has a pencil like this, only me. If you want it, you need to give me your poncho."

"Well, give me the pencil and your detective magnifying glass."

My magnifying glass? I have to decide quickly. Well, I won't be needing it much longer. I dig it out of my pocket and give it to Kevin, who hides it under his desk. Then he puts his pencil case up in front of my face.

"So, will you bring it tomorrow?"

"No way," he says, just as the teacher returns with her coffee. I usually like the smell of coffee from the machine, but it stings my nose today and makes my right eye water, like when I'm tired and tears come out. Only I'm not tired, I'm furious, and I couldn't care less about the pencil or the poncho anymore. All I want is to shut my eyes and draw a giant line through everyone—except Estella and Ottimo Turcaret—and everything, except my tree.

My tree.

Every now and then I think about what it will be like living in it, and I imagine a house made of leaves beside the birds' nests. The cherry tree always has lots of birds' nests. When I'm feeling lonely, I'll knock on the trunk, and I'll hear Grandma's voice say, *Who's there?*

Mafalda! I'll reply, and the cherry tree, or rather the giant, will shake his head to make some pink and white flowers fall around us, and me and Grandma will play guess-what-shapes-the-clouds-are.

But I'm going to need my Sherlock Holmes magnifying glass. I don't feel right without it, and it was a present from Dad. I can't go to the tree without something to remember Dad by.

The bell rings for lunch, and the teacher follows us all out of the classroom. Kevin bolts out double-quick and goes to hide in the bathroom. I lean against the wall near our classroom door, arms folded, and sink to the floor, letting my back slide down the wall. I saw someone do it in a movie. I realize it's been ages since I last watched a movie, and there's little chance I'll see many more before—or after—I end up in the dark. I hide my face between my knees and start to cry.

"Why are you crying?"

Sugary crumbs that smell sweet fall on my hands. I look up. I see a pair of sneakers and two legs in jeans. It could be anyone, but I recognize the voice.

Filippo sits down on the ground beside me and listens while I tell him what happened with Kevin. If I talk too much, Filippo stops listening. I learned that after I got to know him, so I try to give him a quick summary.

He jumps to his feet before I finish the last sentence. He throws his croissant wrapper in the trash, which I think is quite far away, and congratulates himself on his aim, then makes a move toward my classroom.

I get up too and squeeze the hand he has on the door handle really tightly. We're not allowed into the classroom during break. "What are you going to do?"

He pushes me out of the way, gently but firmly. "Help you get your things back. Stay here and tell me if someone comes."

I try to stop him because I'm scared I won't see anyone coming in time and we'll get found out, but Filippo darts into the classroom as quick as lightning and starts rummaging through all the backpacks. I'm half in, half out of the classroom and can feel my stomach lurching in fear. "Under the desk. The desk behind mine, look underneath!"

I don't need to tell him which desk is mine. I see he goes to the right one.

A hand on my shoulder. "What's going on here?"

One of the older teachers, whom I don't know very well, is standing behind me and looking into our classroom. I'm so scared I can't move. Someone else comes over to see what's going on.

"What are you doing?" the teacher asks Filippo, speaking over my head. Filippo is still kneeling, hidden between the desks, but it's too late; they've seen us. Then there's a scream from behind the teacher. "That stuff's mine! They're stealing it!"

Kevin pushes me aside, runs to his desk, and starts yanking Filippo to get the pencil and my magnifying glass back. Filippo won't let go. "They're not yours. You took them from Mafalda; they belong to her!"

"She gave them to me! They're mine now!"

"You tricked me!"

While they shout and yank, even throw the odd punch, the deputy headmaster arrives and splits them up. He demands to know what's going on. Kevin shouts that Filippo started it, that he was stealing Kevin's things, so I start yelling that the things were mine.

"But you gave them to me, you idiot!"

I've no idea what comes over me, but I throw myself at Kevin's stupid voice and end up without my glasses, throwing punches, some of which land in mid-air, some on something soft, hopefully Kevin's face. So, fighting is something I can do without glasses. I must remember to add that to my new list.

The hard chairs in the corridor beside the school office are as uncomfortable as the ones Doctor Olga has, only this time I don't have Mom and Dad with me but Filippo, who also has a behavior note to be signed by the principal and his parents.

It's the first time that I've ever been sent to the principal. And that I've stolen something. I've done lots of things this year that I promised at confession I'd never do. I had no choice, though. I didn't want to behave so badly. I didn't want to run away from home, and I definitely didn't mean to hit Kevin. Okay, so maybe I did want to hit Kevin, but he tricked me, and I hate it when people don't tell me the truth.

"I know you don't like lies, but I'm going to have to tell one in a minute, so you shut up, okay?" Filippo touches my arm gently. What lie do I have to tell? I don't like lies. Always the truth, Estella says. "If I don't say this thing, you'll end up in trouble too, so just zip it."

I push my glasses up my nose and stare at him. "What?"

"Nothing." Filippo swings his legs under the chair. "Say nothing. Want a game of ball-in-the-basket?"

He scrunches the demerit note into a ball and throws it at a fake plant in the corner of the corridor, near the photocopier. There must be a basket over there. I hear his ball plop into it. "You try."

Since I have nothing to throw but the note, I scrunch mine up too. I may as well; I'm already in trouble. I throw my ball toward the basket and hear it hit the wall and roll on the ground. I missed. Filippo runs over to retrieve the balls and gives me mine back. "Let's try again."

I'm on my sixth attempt when the principal comes out of his office to sign our notes. "What on earth are you doing?" I don't need my third eye to see that he is really, truly angry with us.

My courage vanishes, wrapped up in the paper ball on the floor behind the photocopier. I'm about to confess to this offense too (Isn't that what it's called when you break a rule?), but Filippo steps between me and the principal. "It was my fault."

The principal is a tall, skinny man with thinning hair and light blue veins on his forehead. I remember him. He's not evil; he just spends all his time shut away in his office and doesn't speak to us children much. A bit like the janitor with the sauce stains. Maybe they're secretly friends and get together to talk about us over coffee. No, that's impossible. They're too different. But Filippo and I are different, and we're friends. The principal seems to know Filippo quite well.

"It's my fault. I went into her classroom, she tried to stop me, and then I forced her to play ball-in-the-basket with the note."

It's not true. I want to tell the principal this. I stand up, but he's already facing the other way and walking back into his office, heaving a huge sigh. "This is not good, Filippo, not good at all. I think we should let Mafalda go and you and I have a chat."

Filippo doesn't even look at me, and when I try to stop him, he pulls his arm back and tells me to go away. I follow him almost inside the principal's office. The last thing I see between the door closing and the wall is his glasses.

Filippo is my Garrone, just like in *The Baron in the Trees*.

Only in this case, the headmaster hasn't noticed that Filippo was lying to protect me.

I need to run.

It's been ages since I went running, fast like the wind, like the others who run in the park and on the track.

I look around me. There's no one about, no sign of life by the entrance or in the corridor. I hear a door opening to my left and secretaries laughing. A woman wearing, I think, a very smart black skirt walks past me holding some sheets of paper. She needs to use the photocopier. I hear her press buttons and lower the lid, and then a green light lights up my eyes with electric sparks. I look the other way. The secretary asks me if I need anything. I start walking toward my classroom. I can't do anything for Filippo here.

The secretary picks up the balls of paper and retreats

into her office. I hear the door close. I really am the only one in the school now. I stand absolutely still and count to ten in my head. No one goes past; no one comes looking for me. So I make a dash for Estella's room. I only have to cross the big space where we do recitals. The floors in my school are light blue, the walls are gray, and the doors light blue and gray. It's like running through nothingness. I come to a stop with a bang, my whole body slamming into the door of the janitors' room. I open it, go inside, and shut it hastily behind me. I stand with my back against it, heart thudding in my chest like my cousin Andrea's bongo drum.

To calm myself down, I look around, even though my glasses are dirty and blurred, or maybe it's my eyes that are dirty and blurred, like the windshield on Mom's car. I could use some wipers to clean away the dirt. But they haven't invented such small ones yet. The room is in darkness—no one has opened the blinds. There's only a very beautiful shaft of light pouring through one of the small windows that looks out onto the playground.

I place my hand into the shaft of light and play with the dust, moving it around, then open my white hand to see the straighter-than-straight shadows that appear behind my fingers. Light and dark things are all that I can see now, although it's easier when they're side by side. Keeping my hand inside the shaft of light, I move around and try to follow the shadow my hand casts on objects in the room—the swivel chair, the desk, the chips cupboard.

My birthday present! Estella told me she was going to leave it in here. I kneel down under the desk and open the confiscated-property drawer. Feeling around with my hands, I find a paper parcel tied with a crumpled ribbon. I pull it out and place it on the desk. It's a soft, odd-looking parcel.

It's the second time in not very long that I've been given something soft. I wonder what it is.

I sit on the swivel chair and very slowly unwrap the parcel. I definitely don't want to ruin the wrapping paper. But I can't resist and end up ripping it off. A star. That's the first thing I see. A large, white star. Made of fabric, because it's printed on a T-shirt, a black T-shirt, like the ones Filippo's mom makes in her shop. Maybe Estella ordered it from there. The thought of Filippo and Estella being connected makes me very happy. I bury my face in the T-shirt. Estella has washed and ironed it with the same washing powder she uses for her own clothes; I can smell her perfume. The star is a bit shiny—I can also see it with my fingers. They see another star too, a smaller one on the front of the T-shirt. I turn it round and hold it up against me. The smaller star, white like the first one, is right over my heart.

18

No One Shot It

It's always really hot in Mom's car.

It's even hotter today because I have to tell her about the demerit note and how I crumpled it up and threw it away.

But she's chatting away as usual, so I let her speak. I rest my forehead against the window, breathe out on the glass, and draw a star with my finger. It vanishes almost immediately, before I get time to look at it. It doesn't matter. I have Estella's T-shirt in my bag, and there are two stars on that, one for me and another bigger one for her. At home, I hide it under the bed so I can take it with me to the tree, and when spring comes I'll put it on and Estella will have three stars just for her (including the one in her name—she told me once "stella" means "star").

I go up the stairs to our apartment and think that maybe I should call Estella to thank her before I tell Mom and Dad about the demerit note because I might not be allowed to use the phone after. When I climb stairs, I'm always really careful, especially somewhere new, because you never know how high each step might be. At home, my feet go up by themselves. I've been climbing them since I was born, or not long after, so I could do them with my eyes shut. Or in the dark. That's something else to add to the new list.

"Watch out, young lady, make way, make way!"

A talking wardrobe nearly runs me down, but I jump out of the way, into the handrail on the wall, just in time. A walking, talking wardrobe. And it has just come out of my house. "Where are you going?" I ask.

The head of a sweaty man pops out from behind the wardrobe. The sweaty man puts the wardrobe down, so I'm stuck between the handrail and the wardrobe. He is so close to me, I can feel the heat from him. I see him rooting around in his pockets for something. A sheet of paper. He looks at it and says, "Twenty-Three Via Gramsci. That's where I'm going."

He picks up the wardrobe again and, with great difficulty, resumes his journey down the stairs.

I run home and trip over a box in front of the door. "Wha—"

"Mafalda, be careful, darling."

"Mom, what's happening?"

Mom comes out of the kitchen with a saucepan lid in her hand and her bag still over her shoulder.

"We've started moving. Don't you remember the new house? You saw it too. We have to start taking our things there because we're moving in next week."

I reach out to touch the chest of drawers by the front door, the one with Mom and Dad's wedding picture on it, but my hand swings straight across without touching anything. There's only air and gray light where the drawers used to be. They've taken it away. I wonder if they put the photo safely into a box. I'd be sad if they broke it. I like that photo, even though I can no longer see it very well.

Misted glasses alert. I head for my room. Boxes are stacked up in the hallway. I have to be careful not to bump into them because they're not an easy color to see. An ugly color, to be honest, the color of recycled toilet paper. Mom follows me holding the pan lid. I look at her over my shoulder, and for a second, I'm not even sure it's her.

"Mom, can I go to my room on my own?"

"All right, on you go. Be careful where you put your feet. I'll call you when the pasta's ready."

I stand in the doorway. It's dark in my room. All I

have to do is reach out with my hand to turn on the light, but I shut my eyes. I take one step into the room, then another, until I know I'm in the middle. I turn round slowly. And I know. I know everything is still in its place, that nothing has been moved or removed yet. As I swing round, I can feel the presence of things on my hands and on my face. I'm in no doubt. The furniture is where it has always been, as are my things. This is the last room they'll empty. I walk toward my wardrobe, brush my hand against it. The wood is light-colored, I know. Another two steps and I'm at my desk. So that's where I left my sharpener—I couldn't find it at school. There's a loose tile on the floor, one that moves a little. There it is. When I walk on it, the fake crystals on the ceiling light, above my head and over to the left a bit, make a barely perceptible tinkling noise. The last time I looked at myself in the mirror, I stood right here. I open my eyes. Where the mirror used to be, there's nothing.

I move closer. One step. Another. And another. Maybe my mirror was the only thing they took away, you know, to get started. I hardly have time to put out my hand to check where the mirror is when there's a bang and it explodes into a thousand pieces. It was there, right there, and now . . . I've cut myself. The blood smells like house keys.

"Mafalda, what happened?" Mom comes scream-ing from the kitchen, then screams even louder when she sees the broken glass and my blood. "Stay right there. I'll get something to put on it."

She runs to the bathroom. I hear her rummaging through cupboards, the ones that are left.

I broke the mirror. I bumped into it; it fell over and smashed.

Okay, we've reached no steps from the mirror. It's Wednesday today. On Monday, I'm moving, or rather, they're moving, to the new house. Because in three days' time I'll be in the tree and won't be coming down again.

Voices from the kitchen wake me up. Someone's cry-ing and talking to Mom. It's morning. The mist isn't thick yet, so I need to take advantage of it. I want to know who came to visit so early in the morning.

First things first, I stick my feet into my slippers—I wouldn't want to tread on a shard of broken glass—and then I go into the kitchen, watching out for fur-niture that's been moved and boxes stacked up in the hall.

"Good morning, Mafalda. Sorry if I woke you."

Ravina's voice and the jet-black of her hair. "What are you doing here?" I ask her.

Mom has me sit down at the table and gives me a mug of tea and a muffin. "Ravina came to say good-bye. She's going back to India for a while."

I almost spill all my tea on the tablecloth—what a disaster that would've been. I push my glasses up my nose and look at Ravina, mouth agape. "Why are you leaving? When are you coming back?"

She sighs. Her eyes are dark, like when Mom forgets to take off her makeup and the next morning she looks like the panda I once saw at the zoo. I'm almost certain this is what happens when grown-up women cry.

"Andrea and I have broken up. I'm going back to live with my grandparents. I'll help them around the house and they'll keep me company."

"Why have you broken up?"

"Mafalda, Ravina might not want to talk about it."

Ravina pats my arm gently and tells Mom it's okay, that she actually came to spend some time with me. Mom warns me not to harass her, then starts washing last night's dishes. I'm still not used to her being at home all the time. I keep thinking she'll go to work any minute, but she doesn't, and she is here to constantly check up on me.

Ravina explains that it was her decision to split with Andrea because he never tells her that he cares about her. I'm not sure I understand, so I ask, "Isn't caring about someone what you say to your mom and dad, your relatives, your friends, your pet, people like that? Whereas boyfriend and girlfriend are supposed to say 'I love you,' except for in France, where they say *Je t'aime* to everyone. The assistant French teacher told me that."

"That's true, and he never told me he loves me either."

"Not even in French?"

"No, not even in French. I told him that I love him at least a hundred times."

No way! Ravina said I love you a hundred times! I need to warn her!

"But you'll have a hundred babies!"

"What's this about babies, Mafalda?" Mom turns to look at me, confused.

"Nothing, it's just that after someone tells someone else they love them, a baby comes."

"Who told you that?"

"No one." I don't want Estella to get the blame, because I think I've got this baby thing mixed up. In fact, Ravina explains that it's much more difficult to have a baby, that just saying "I love you" is not enough. On the contrary, if you love someone and don't say I love you, not only will you not have babies, but you'll also lose the other person, the way Andrea has lost her.

Mom makes coffee for her and Ravina, and I get washed and dressed for school. Dad helps me put on my backpack and opens the front door. Ravina comes to hug me. She smells of church again, but also of water and the beach. It's the smell of someone who's been crying. If you ask me, everyone has a special smell when they've been crying, and she smells of water and the beach. She squeezes me tight, then takes my face between her hands and brings her eyes almost inside mine, so I can see them nearly perfectly. They're not black. They are deep, deep brown. "Never ever give up, Mafalda. Don't forget that."

"Okay. Never ever give up."

"You're a brave frog."

She goes out onto the landing. My glasses mist up as I say goodbye. It's the last time I'll see Ravina before she goes to India. She might never come back, and even if she does, I'll be in the dark in the cherry tree by then.

19

This Is Interesting

"Look how many flowers there are on the cherry tree, Mafalda."

I'm walking to school with my hand squeezed tight in Dad's. I look at the cherry tree and pretend for a moment that I'm meditating upon the beauty of the flowers, like Ravina told me once. She's really good at meditating, which means thinking really hard. In truth, we're still too far away. Dad still says things like "Did you see?" and "look there" and "see that," and I feel bad because he's always so happy to show me things, so I say nothing, but then after a bit he realizes what he's just said and gets sad, and I think he'd like to say sorry. So I say, "Wait till we get a bit closer," and when I see, both of us are happy again.

This worked until not so long ago, but now I can hardly see any of what Dad points to, not even when we get closer. The early spring blossoms must be out on the cherry tree today. I try to do as Ravina suggested, so I shut my eyes and breathe deeply. Right away my nostrils feel cold inside, but when the air hits me, I can smell it: the scent of spring. For me, it smells of Grandma's rhubarb sweets and of bunches of flowers—not the ones at the florist's shop that smell like a graveyard when they're all squished together, but real flowers, wild ones growing in fields and in the gardens of kind old ladies.

It's time to count because I'm pretty sure I can see something that looks like a tree with flowers. One of my gray clouds is blurring the school, but I'm sure my tree is waiting for me right next to it, flowers lining its branches. I remember what cherry blossoms look like in spring—lots of little balls, or thousands of white butterflies curled up on the giant's head after the winter vacation.

So, even though I'm not sure I can see clearly, I start counting—one step, two steps, three . . . The closer I get to school, the more I inhale the fresh scent of spring that smells like sweets. The air on my face, in my hair, feels like the brush of the blue silk scarf of a smiling lady. A wisp of hair tickles my nose, but I don't flick it away. I count the steps and get to fifty-two. I'm twenty-six meters from the tree. Twenty-six, bending the rules slightly. It still counts, doesn't it, if the balled-up flowers and the tree that I saw are not strictly real, just the way I remember them?

I have to think about this. Ravina said we have to be honest with ourselves. I don't know what this means, but I think it has something to do with the truth. Don't tell lies, not even in your head. I look down at the ground while I think about the lies-in-your-head thing, until a faint, almost inaudible whistle draws my attention to the school stairs. It sounds like Estella's secret call, only much shorter than usual.

I let go of Dad's hand and run up the stairs, passing close to the cherry tree. I smell the fresh scent of the bark even if I don't touch it.

"Estella! You're back!"

"Yes . . ."

Going up the school steps comes naturally to me, like at home, but all of a sudden I realize I'm alone—no Dad's hand, or Estella's, not yet anyway—and I miscount the number of stairs. There are seventeen in total. I usually take them two at a time, except for the first one, so I don't leave a single stair at the end and mess up my rhythm. Never mind, I'm usually okay about going up the school steps, even that time I left my glasses in Mom's car and Grandma brought them to school for me during second period—I wasn't afraid then. I am today. I know how big a step I have to take to get up to the next stair, but it's like my foot seems to have forgotten everything, and instead of the stairs under me, there's only lava with crocodiles in it, and if I fall in, they'll eat me, and I'll die, boiled alive.

"Ah!"

I lose my balance, tilt backward, fall. The anticipation of falling into the mist is awful. But I don't fall. Estella's strong hands grab me by the arms and pull; they pull me up the last stair, the top one where she's standing, and I stumble straight into her, glasses on the end of my nose, face squashing into her perfumed overalls.

It's the first time we've hugged like this. Mom hugs me all the time. Grandma would pick me up even if she had sore arms and legs. But there's something different about Estella. Mom's hugs are soft at the front, like a pillow. Grandma's were too. It was like she had cake mix spread over her heart.

Estella is only like that on one side—on the other, where her heart is, you can hear it go *boom, boom,*

boom, but there's nothing else. I lift my face to hers to ask what happened, but from the bottom of the stairs, Dad's voice is asking if I'm all right. Estella breaks away and turns me round to show him I'm all in one piece.

We go into school. She doesn't resume the hug, and I struggle to speak to her. My third eye gives me some good advice—leave it until lunch. In the doorway to my classroom, I ask Estella if I can come see her later.

She pats my head with her strong hand, and she's like the smiling lady in the air from before, the one with the blue silk scarf, not Estella, Queen of the Amazons.

"What happened on the stairs this morning?" Estella asks me later.

"What are you doing?"

The room is a mess. The light pouring through the small window is full of dust, and my fingers feel objects on every surface I touch. Even my shoes bump against something on the ground near my feet, books perhaps.

Estella brushes the dust from my nose with a cloth sprayed full of glass cleaner, the same one Mom uses. "You really are a little princess, aren't you? When you want to know something, you don't stop to listen to other people's questions."

"Sorry. What are you doing?"

Estella folds up the cloth, exhales, and pushes the swivel chair over to me.

I sit down and spin.

"I'm cleaning, my dear. It needs doing occasionally."

"I know. My bedroom also needs cleaning. But I've got ablutophobia."

Estella smiles—I can hear it in her voice. "And what's ablutophobia?"

I clasp the desk to bring the chair to a stop. "I don't know. I read it in a book once. I think it's when you can't do something you don't want to do anyway."

"Ah, I get it. That can happen."

It occurs to me that as we speak, a sweaty man might be in the bedroom that I never clean, removing the wardrobe, the desk, the bed, and I've left Grandma's blanket under the bed, with all the things I need inside it. If I were grown up, I'd tell Mom and Dad that moving to a new house is not that bad, which for me means utterly, horribly bad.

"Estella?"

My Amazon queen sits on a stool and sighs again. "What?"

"Are you ever afraid?"

I hear her put her hands on her hips. She and Filippo do it in almost exactly the same way.

"Of course. I get afraid sometimes. It's normal."

"So, what do you do?"

"I think. I look for a solution. And if I can't find one, I think of something nice, something fun that makes me happy, and I stop being scared."

"And when you're really, really scared?"

"Mafalda, fear isn't always a bad thing, you know."

"Why not?"

"Sometimes things happen that scare you a lot. . . ."

"Like moving to a new house, for example? Or being in the dark?"

"Yes, exactly, like moving to a new house or being in the dark. The fear you feel about them makes you stop and think, and it's only by thinking them through that people grow bigger, stronger."

"More muscular, you mean?"

Estella smiles, but she's tired. She smells of pillow (pillows always have a special smell) and of winter cherry. "No, Mafalda, not muscular, but brave. Strong in your head. With the passing of time, fear helps you to see things more clearly."

"Fear helps me to see better?" Interesting.

I hear Estella stand up and move to the middle of the room. "Come here," she says.

I kick forward on the swivel chair to reach her.

"Stand up."

I stand up. This is one of those times that I feel afraid, when the smile disappears from Estella's voice. I'm in front of her, standing up. What now?

She puts her hands, all hard again, on my shoulders and pulls me toward her. She hugs me tight, and I hug her back. It comes as naturally as climbing the stairs at home. My temple and cheek sink into her overalls, and I feel the same *boom, boom, boom* coming from where the soft cushion should be, the one that makes the heart more muffled.

I inspect Estella from her feet up. Her face is almost completely covered by my gray cloud, but I can see a bit of her lips—she forgot her lipstick this morning—and her hair, as dark and black as usual.

"Do you want to know why I'm like this?"

I'm not sure what to say. I'm scared I might upset her somehow, or make her angry. "Like what?" I splutter.

She snorts, takes one of my hands, and presses it against her overalls, over the chest pocket.

I try to pull my hand away, but Estella holds it firmly in place under her own. "What can you feel?"

"Nothing!"

"That's not true. What can you feel?"

I feel that I've gone bright red and nervous; I feel

my heart beating like a bongo drum . . . and hers, too. I calm down and listen better with my hand. Estella's heart is beating like a bongo drum. Just like mine.

"What can you feel?"

I look at her again. And smile. "Your heart."

"See? You were afraid, but you stopped to let your head grasp it, and then the truth wasn't so bad, was it?"

"No." Estella lets my hand go. "Where did it go?"

She doesn't answer; maybe she doesn't understand.

"The soft stuff that should be there." I point to her heart.

"Ah, right, the other half. Well, my friend took it away."

"The one you saw in the hospital?"

"Yes."

"She's not nice."

"You're right; she's not nice doing this to me. But I've thought and thought about it, and I know what to do if she comes back to see me."

"Have you made a plan?"

Her smile returns. "You could say that. What about you? Do you have a plan?"

I go up close to her again and gesture for her to kneel down, so I can put my hands up to her ear and whisper my secret plan. "My plan is to go and live in the cherry tree in front of the school."

Estella thinks about it for a second, then shrugs her shoulders. "I think that's an excellent plan. Let me know when you go. I'll help with the move."

Then she shoos me out of her room as she has to ring the bell for the end of break. When the door closes, I'm in the thick of the chaos, people running, shouting, blowing bubbles into their fruit juice, and I'm reminded of the story of the Amazons, their courage, how they cut off a boob to hold their spears better. That's what Estella said. I turn toward the little window of the janitors' room, the one that looks inside the school, and I think I see her scary eyes, peeping out and smiling at me from between the slats of the lowered blinds, only they're not scary; they're just black and beautiful. Then my mist comes and covers them up, or maybe Estella lowered the blinds so no one will find out she's a real Amazon.

I Breathe

I open my eyes.

All children are scared of the dark. I am too, because for me, the dark is a blindfold you put over your eyes to play a game but can't take off when the game's over.

I blink again and again. Over there, where the window should be, with the moon and the North Star inside it, or the sun during the day, I can't see anything. My room is gray. If I wave my hand in front of me, it's gray too. The dark is gray. It's so much worse than black, I think.

Ottimo Turcaret is brown and gray. Maybe I'll still be able to see the things that were gray before the dark came. But I can't feel his warmth on my feet. I touch my slippers at the bottom of the bed with one hand. He's not there, either.

"Mom!"

Breathe, Mafalda. Remember to breathe. A nice smell of coffee and sponge cake is coming from the kitchen. Dad must've bought one at the market, given that there's practically nothing left in our house because of the move.

"What's up, Mafalda? It's a bit early to get up. You can stay in bed and I'll call you in a bit."

"Where's Ottimo Turcaret?"

Mom moves around my room. I can hear her bare feet, the air moving as she passes close to me, the creaking noise of a plastic bag and the soft swish of clothes picked up and put into it.

A bead of sweat runs down my forehead and stops by my ear. I have to pretend nothing's wrong because if Mom finds out I'm in the dark, she'll never let me go anywhere today, maybe never, and she'll force me to go to the new house, and I don't know where things are there.

"Where's Ottimo Turcaret?" I insist.

"In a boarding house for animals. Dad took him

last night, while he was sleeping. You know nothing wakes him up."

Guesthouse for animals? What does that mean? Cats go to guesthouses too? Maybe it's one of those places grandparents go to when they have no one left. But Ottimo Turcaret has me, so why have they sent him to a guesthouse?

"Why didn't you take him to Aunt and Uncle's?"

"Oh, they weren't that keen on looking after the cat. But don't worry, it's only temporary, until we've finished the move."

I don't want to speak to Mom anymore. I can't see her, so I can pretend she's not here and not talk to her. I pull the covers back up and try to cry quietly, with my body, not my voice, the way Filippo does, while Mom keeps moving around, and I feel the bed vibrate ever so gently with each of her steps.

Filippo. I need to speak to Filippo. I'm going to the cherry tree today. I can't wait any longer. The dark has come, and I have to try to climb up before the monsters grab my feet and take me away. But I also want to tell Filippo that we're still friends, we can still be a band, I can sing from the tree, and if I'm brave enough, maybe I'll even say "I love you" so he'll never go away.

Good, I'm going, then. As soon as the house goes

completely quiet, I sit very still on the edge of my bed, feet resting on my slippers. It feels like I'm on a roller coaster, at the very top, just before it launches into the first drop, when you throw your arms up and shut your eyes. But I don't go down. Ever. I think I'm about to be sick. I'll have to get used to it. I breathe. I start to reach for my glasses, but what's the point? I don't need them anymore. But I have to convince Mom and Dad that everything is okay. Better put them on. I reach out to the shelf where I lay my glasses at night, but I've been too hesitant. I knock them over and they fall. I stop to listen. No reaction to the noise from the kitchen. I hear teaspoons tinkling against the sides of coffee cups and Dad yawning like a hippo. All good. I feel about on the ground, find my glasses, and put them on without stopping to think where my face is. Okay, this is important—in the dark you just have to get on with things; don't stop to think too much. But I'm afraid, and Estella said that when you're scared, you should stop and think.

I don't think this technique is going to work for me. What was the other one? Oh yeah, think about something nice. The cherry tree.

I reach under the bed and pull out Grandma's blanket with all my things in it: Roly's pink lunch box, Chiara's blow-up mattress, the iPod, some clean underwear and socks because Mom always says, "Think how embarrassing it would be if something were to happen to you and you're taken to the hospital with dirty socks and dirty underwear." Kevin never gave me back my Sherlock Holmes magnifying glass, so I'll have to do without it. The same goes for the waterproof jacket. I'll take the little umbrella Mom keeps in her bicycle basket down in the garden.

I quickly feel all my things with my fingers to check that I've not forgotten anything. I tie the corners of the blanket together and shove the bundle into the bottom of my backpack. My pencil case and the books I need for school today are on a chair near the bed. I got them all ready last night because my desk has already been taken to the new house. I put them on top of the bundle to hide it. I shut my backpack and hope that it looks the same as every other day and not like I'm about to run away from home.

Before I go, I feel for my notebook. I'd really like to see the list of things that I care a lot about but won't be able to do anymore, but how can I read it? I should've written it in braille dots. I can only touch the page now, feel the dust on the surface, the folds, and my heart beating inside the tips of my fingers. At least I know there are still two things on the list, two things I haven't crossed out with black pen: *Climbing up the school cherry tree*, and on the second page, *Be strong like an Amazon*. Maybe it's too late, because I feel so tired. I don't want to be strong like an Amazon anymore; it's too hard. The dark is here, and all I want is to climb the cherry tree. I don't care about the distance between me and the tree anymore.

21

I Didn't Even Say Goodbye to Ottimo Turcaret

Estella told me to let her know when I go to the cherry tree. She wants to give me a hand, and I think I'm going to need it. Very soon, I'll hear her whistle, and everything will be fine; she'll help me up the stairs, we'll agree to meet under the tree at break, and then when the others go back into the classroom, I'll say goodbye, I'll let her give me a leg up, and I'll climb the cherry tree for the last time.

I dress slowly, not too slowly or Mom will come check on me. Too bad Mom picked today to leave me out a blouse. The buttons are difficult in the dark. But my fingers like the buttons; they're smooth and cool and slip quickly into the right slots. Maybe one didn't. I'll just have to hope Mom doesn't check. She comes into my room to do my pigtails. Singing to herself. I haven't told her about the demerit note I got with Filippo. I may as well keep it to myself now. I'll be gone soon.

I take lots of deep breaths on the way to school, so many that after a while, Dad asks me if I'm feeling all right.

I need to calm down. It's just that I didn't even say goodbye to Ottimo Turcaret. I don't know where he is. The only thing I know is that I'll never see him again when I am in the tree, and this fills my eyes with tears.

Dad mustn't hear me cry or he'll realize something's wrong. I squeeze his hand and point to the cherry tree, even though I'm not completely sure it's where I'm pointing. I risk it. "The giant and Grandma have stuck their prettiest flowers to the branches, haven't they, Dad?"

It's spring. We talked about flowers yesterday, and I can smell rhubarb sweets on the morning breeze. "They have indeed," Dad replies, and squeezes my hand back.

Poor Dad. In his favorite book, it's the father's fault that Cosimo goes to live in the trees, or that's what I understood. Cosimo's dad was too strict and made him eat all the rubbish food that Cosimo's sister used to cook. My dad is fairly kind, even though he forces me to eat tuna, and it was his decision to make us move to a new house. I'll write him a letter from the tree to explain everything.

"We're here," he says, and I almost bump straight into the tree trunk. Estella didn't whistle.

"Your friendly janitor doesn't seem to be here today. I'll take you inside," Dad says, and I hear him moving toward the stairs already.

"No, it's fine. I'll go up myself."

I start going up the steps, my heart pounding under my sweater, under the small white printed star. Wearing Estella's T-shirt under my blouse seemed like the best way of bringing it with me.

"Are you sure?"

"Yes. Bye," I say, without turning round.

"Okay. Bye. See you later."

I get to the door and follow the others into the classroom, running one hand along the wall, trying not to draw attention to myself so the teachers don't notice. Luckily, we don't have any tests today, and Fernando leaves me alone. He just helps me sort my folders and books—thank goodness we don't take too many notes today—and he switches on the computer

I use to practice playing the recorder during our music lesson. I'm a bit scared when we play, but Filippo's right; music is my friend, and even if I can't see the notes on the computer, I can still play the songs we've done hundreds of times together in class. No one says anything.

I don't know what to do at lunch and recess. I try to stand still as much as I can so I don't attract the teacher's attention, while I wonder where Estella is, today of all days, when I need her help. I hear the voice of the janitor with the stained shirt as he walks past me. He's on his phone.

"So sorry."

He stops speaking into the phone, and I realize he's annoyed. "What's up?"

"Where's Estella?"

"How should I know? She's always sick, that one, and I get landed with all her work."

"Is she sick?"

"What's it to you? Are you her daughter?"

"No. My name's Mafalda."

The voice of the janitor with the stained shirt changes. "Mafalda, you said?"

"Yes."

"Your friend left you a letter. Wait here while I get it for you."

He moves away, talking on his phone, and I follow his voice. Someone bumps into me, and I hope it's Filippo, but I think he's in detention in his classroom. It happens. Quite a lot.

"Here you are. On you go now, back to your classroom; the bell's about to ring."

I'm holding Estella's letter in my hands. It's an envelope with a sheet of paper folded in half inside, so it's a short letter. What does she have to write that she can't say in person? Someone will have to help me read the letter, and quick, because my third eye is shouting as loud as it can that maybe this sheet says where Estella is and what's wrong with her. I need to find Filippo.

"Mom, can you take me to Filippo's house today?"

"Not today, Mafalda. We have to finish packing and moving our things."

We're in the car, and I'm so agitated, I forgot to put my glasses back on after gym. Fernando made me do silly exercises while the others were doing hurdles, and my glasses are still in his pocket. My backpack is half-empty because I left the blanket containing my things in the locker room at the gym so it's ready for later. School is open until six o'clock in the afternoon for pupils who do clubs and sports—I'll be able to go in and get my bundle to take it with me to the tree.

Only everything's going wrong. "But I've still got one day left!"

"Until what?" Mom asks, genuinely surprised at how loud I'm yelling.

"The new house!"

"I know, but wouldn't it be better if we could get there a bit earlier? That way you can arrange your room, meet the neighbors, and . . ."

I stop listening to her. If we finish the move today, I'm done for. I've got no choice. I have to sneak out, go to Filippo's, get him to read me the letter, find out where Estella is, then climb up the tree before Mom and Dad find me.

22

Climbing up the School Cherry Tree

More men who smell of sweat and dust and cardboard walk near me, and the more they talk to each other as they move the last few boxes, the more I realize the house is empty. Their voices echo off the walls, the boxes make the floor shake, and it makes me want to put my hands over my ears. But I can't—it would give my secret away.

I'd like to phone Filippo on Mom's phone to tell him to come here and read me Estella's letter, but I can't find it in all the chaos and nothingness left in the house, and with the darkness that's in my eyes. In the end, I can't stand it any longer and head in the direction of Mom's voice as she tells the sweaty men to put her bike in the truck as well.

"Mom, can you read me something?"

Mom is fanning herself with something that smells like old newspaper. "Mafalda, I don't have time right now. Can't you use your magnifying glass?"

"I left it at school."

She comes over to me, very, very close, and moves my hair out of my face. My pigtails unraveled a little during gym. She wants to know if everything is okay. I'm scared she's looking into my eyes and can see that the light has gone off. What am I supposed to do when I'm scared? Think of something nice. The cherry tree. I crack a huge smile and turn round so Mom can comb my hair. She relaxes. "So, what do you want me to read to you?"

I give her Estella's letter, and she opens it and lays it on my head. "Oh, what big writing! They've used a marker pen, just the way you like it. I think you could read it yourself, even without your magnifying glass."

"I don't have my glasses. Sorry. You do it, please."

"Oh, okay. Here we go. 'Dear Mafalda—a while ago I told you that a not-nice friend of mine took away a bit of me, do you remember? Well, Estella does not tell lies. Only truth. So, I think you should know that it wasn't a friend, but a very nasty illness, and the illness has come back, and now it's trying to take away another bit of me, maybe even all of me. That's why I'm in the hospital and couldn't do our secret whistle. . . .' Oh, Mafalda, I'm so sorry!"

Mom stops reading, and her voice is terribly, terribly sad, but my head is so full of words cartwheeling around that I don't understand any of it. With my eyes stinging, I grab the letter out of Mom's hand. "Enough!"

I run from Mom's voice, she shouts, "Where are you going?" and I shout that I want to be alone, please; by pure coincidence I manage to find my room, gather up my notebook from where I'd left it behind the door, rip out the first few pages, the list and everything, then run out of the front door, down the stairs, almost killing myself, through the door into the garden where I hear Dad's voice, very near to me, telling me to slow down and not go too far.

I lean against the fence round the back to catch my breath. I hate running in the dark. And even if I promised I'd never say it, I'm going to now—I hate, hate, hate, hate, hate, hate, hate, hate it! I hate it all: I hate the new house, I hate school, hate grandparents because they die, hate cats because they disappear and can't get down cherry trees, hate boyfriends because they don't say "I love you," and hate myself because everyone else can see and I can't.

"Hey, are you all right?"

An unfamiliar voice. On the other side of the road. The horrible neighbors who live in Grandma's house.

"Why did you take her curtains down?!" I'm just as shocked as they are at my screams, and tears run into my mouth—I hadn't realized I was crying so hard. I feel for the bolt on the fence, open it, pull the gate toward me, and run outside onto the pavement, where Filippo stopped with his bike to chat and stroke Ottimo Turcaret. His apartment is not that far from my house. When I get to the T-shirt printing shop, I'll scream at the top of my voice for Filippo. He'll come down into the street and help me get to the hospital, because I have to tell Estella what my essential thing is. Maybe if I tell her, she won't go and live in the tree with Grandma and the giant. If I tell her what's essential for me, she'll stay here and help me climb up the tree and maybe explain why cats can't get down trees.

I try to walk quickly on the pavement and not lose my way. I drag one hand along the walls of the houses and garden gates. *Oww!* Pain really hurts in the dark because you're not expecting it. A splinter gets stuck under the nail of my middle finger, which I think is the most painful thing of all, but I can't start crying again; I haven't got time. I need to keep going. I think I've touched this wall already; I recognize the lumps of paint. I must be going around our neighborhood in circles, and have been for a while.

The sound of a car that makes the same noise as Mom's comes from the end of the street. It's getting closer. I kneel down on the ground so they won't see me, although I have no idea if there's anything in front of me to hide me. I hide my face in my arms. The car goes past and doesn't stop. I start walking again. A door with a bell opens on my left, and I hear the voices of men and women saying hello and the ting of glasses clinking. I keep going, pretending to be confident and relaxed, even though I've mixed up so many streets and roads, I have no idea where I'm going. After quite a lot of steps, the voice of a woman, who's neither old nor young, asks me something. I'm immersed in all the things worrying me and don't listen.

"Wait! Where are you going all by yourself?"

I try not to look at the woman's face, as she'll realize I'm in the dark and take me straight back to my mom and dad. "I'm going home."

"At this time, all alone? How old are you?"

"Why, what time is it?"

Nothing. The lady must be looking at her watch. "Six o'clock. It's dark."

"Oh no!" I've been out for almost two hours and hadn't realized. It's too late to get Grandma's blanket from the locker in the gym. I'll be lucky if I can even get back to our garden. Okay, the priority now is to get to Estella. I'll deal with the blanket later.

"Where do you live?"

I'd like to tell her to leave me alone and that she's a stranger and I don't tell strangers where I live, but then I think she could help me. "I live near the shop where they print T-shirts, but it's not my house. It's my aunt's. I live somewhere else. Can you help me get to my aunt's? I think I must be lost, and my aunt will be angry if I'm late."

The woman is not convinced. "And what's your aunt's name? Maybe I know her."

"She's called Christine. The T-shirt printing shop is hers. Can you help me get there? My aunt will be angry if —"

"If you're late, I get it. Let's go; it's just round the corner. You were almost there."

The lady takes my hand, and I'm a little scared she might trick me and take me away, but a few steps later she tells me we've arrived and lets go of my hand. "There's the shop you were looking for. Be sure to cross the road at the crosswalk."

I hear cars whizzing past, then a *ding, ding* that I know well. "Filippo!"

The lady talks to the street. "Is that your cousin?"

I say it is and I'm happy, because it looks like my aunt really does live here and the lady can go away.

Filippo's voice, from the other side of the road: "*Ciao*, Mafalda!" He must be just back from his piano lesson.

The lady says goodbye and I step down off the pavement. I'm so happy to be at Filippo's that I forget to listen to the noise and for the air moving. All I hear is his voice shouting, "Mafalda, stop!" then a loud blast from a car horn and a bang, like a box falling and scattering its contents everywhere.

Then only silence. Cars stop going past and people on the pavement stop speaking. Perhaps the world has stopped. I've stopped too, one foot on the road and one foot on the pavement, leg bent back slightly, notebook in my hand. I can't even hear my heart beating under the white star.

The voices of the lady and of other people in the street, in cars, up above me, on balconies, I think, at windows, noises all around me, brisk footsteps, air moving, everything and everyone all mixed together, deafeningly. I drop my notebook, cover my ears to block out Filippo shouting, "Mafalda, Mafalda!" I start running. I run away, bump into a big, foul-smelling box, a trash can. I fall hands-first onto the pavement.

No one bothers with me, so I get up and walk as fast as I can, dragging a hand along the walls, and after who knows how long, instead of tears filling my nose and mouth, the scent of Grandma's rhubarb sweets creeps in, and under my feet I feel the stones of the road outside school. I run to the gate—it's open, silence all around. I go onto the school grounds, wrap my arms round the cherry tree. It feels cool, and with no glasses, no magnifying glass, no North Star, no Ottimo Turcaret, no Estella, no Filippo, I climb, and climb, and climb, and finally I'm up.

Darkness.

In the nighttime in my eyes, everything is dark gray and silent, like a cloud bearing rain. The monsters trying to grab my feet are waiting under the cherry tree. I'm scared I'll fall, but I'm also tired, so very, very tired.

I stretch out on the branch I'm sitting on, rest my damp cheek on it, the branch now wet. I grip with all my might. *Here I am, Grandma. I've come; it's me, Mafalda*, and I fall asleep breathing balled-up flowers and the green hair of the giant.

* * *

See, Cosimo? In the end I came.

You know, I was so sure I'd meet you here, you and Grandma and the giant. Knock, knock, I keep rapping the branch, but no one comes out to keep me company. I should have known you were alone in the trees as well. Maybe it wasn't that great living in the trees after all. So why did you do it? Why have I done it? The branches are hard and uncomfortable, it's cold, and I've left everything I need at home.

Estella always says to think about something nice when you're sad. I concentrate, and right away I think of her, Estella, and I'm tempted to have a nap with a dream, one I've thought about for so long. . . .

23

Be Strong Like an Amazon

Mafalda. Mafalda, wake up."

The voice from below and the pain in my cheek make me open my eyes. It's still all gray, and it's cold, too. I sit up on the branch, rest my back against the trunk, pull my legs into my chest. But the dark is so dark that I lose my balance and don't know what to hold on to; I nearly fall. More tears bubble out slowly from my eyes. I wipe them away with my sleeve. I think of Filippo.

"For goodness' sake, won't you even look at me?"

Estella.

I know it's impossible, but it's like I can see her, so thin in her janitor's overalls, bright pink lipstick, hands on her hips like Filippo, dark eyes rimmed with black.

"Are you not even going to say hello?"

"Sorry. I thought you were in the hospital. I was coming to see you."

She moves a few steps closer to the trunk and leans against it. I feel her touch all the way up here, through the bark. "Well, all you've done is worry your mom and dad. They've been looking for you all night. Luckily, I found you."

"Yes, luckily."

We don't speak for a while. The only sound is a cricket on the branches above me. I love crickets. Unlike cats, they know how to climb down trees, from anywhere high.

I look up and ask, "Estella, do you know why cats can't get down cherry trees?"

Her voice looks up, toward me. "From cherry trees?"

"Yes, from cherry trees. Do you know why?"

Estella sighs. "You're quite a girl; you ask some questions. . . ."

"Do you know why?"

A smile blossoms in her voice. "Of course I do."

"Why? Why can't they?"

"Because it's not in their nature. They have claws to climb up with, and they're attracted to things they might find in trees."

"Like cherries, you mean?"

"More like birds."

"Maybe they like chasing butterflies."

"Maybe."

"Then they can't get down."

"Exactly."

"But why?"

"I told you, Mafalda, they have claws."

"Why don't they jump? Cats can do huge, enormous, gigantic jumps."

"Okay, Mafalda, I'll tell you the truth. Cats don't know how to get down cherry trees because they're scared."

I lean out a little toward her and let my legs swing in the dark. "Scared? Of what?"

"Well, of falling, of killing themselves."

"You mean of dying?"

"Yes."

Silence again. I move my hands over my head, anchoring myself to the branch with my legs, and touch the delicate leaves and silky, soft flowers on my tree. Some of them come off and land on my nose;

others caress my arms and fall to the ground with an almost imperceptible flutter. Very slowly, I ask Estella if she's afraid of dying.

She starts climbing up the cherry tree and makes it shake all over. She stops near my branch.

"Of course I'm afraid. You're afraid of something too, aren't you, Mafalda?"

I play with one of the silk flowers that landed on my hand. "Yes. Of the dark."

"Aren't you in the dark now? You don't seem too scared to me. You climbed up the cherry tree."

I look at her through the gray. Her face is so close, I can nearly see it, I'm sure, nearly.

"How do you know I'm in the dark?"

"Well, I've got a third eye, just like you."

"Are you going to tell my mom and dad?"

"They'll work it out by themselves. They also have a third eye, you know. All moms and dads have them."

I pull my legs in again to my chest. "That's all very well, but I'm not coming down from here."

Estella raps the trunk twice. "That sounds like a good idea. You've got the flowers, the giant, your grandma . . . Have you tried to speak to her?"

"Yes, but . . ."

"She didn't answer, did she?"

"No, but it's nighttime. She'll be sleeping."

"It's nearly morning, Mafalda."

I turn my head away so she doesn't see the tears.

Estella sits on a branch just below mine. "Do you know, Mafalda, there was once a cat that knew how to climb down cherry trees?

"A long time ago, when the Egyptians were building the pyramids, cats were worshipped as gods, and a scribe who worked for the pharaoh decided to teach his cat to climb down cherry trees, because he knew it was a special thing for cats and he wanted to surprise his ruler."

"What color was the cat?"

"It was brown and gray."

"Like Ottimo Turcaret!"

"Yes, like your chubby cat."

"Were there cherry trees in Egypt?"

"Oh yes. They had the tallest, prettiest cherry trees you've ever seen, but they don't have them anymore— they chopped them all down."

"Why?"

"To make room for the pyramids."

"Oh."

"So, I was telling you, the man, the scribe, taught the cat to climb down cherry trees in a very clever way—he would just put the cat in a tree and leave it there."

"What do you mean, leave it there? In the cherry tree?"

"Yes. One time, he left it in the last cherry tree still standing. The pyramid was almost finished, and the cherry tree was right where they wanted to build."

"So, what did they do with the cat? They didn't pull the tree down with the cat in it?"

"Worse. That was what they wanted to do, but since it was the prettiest tree in all of Egypt, at the last minute they decided not to chop it down and to build the pyramid around and over it, and if the cat didn't want to come down, worse for him."

"That can't be true."

Estella laughs. "Well, guess what? The cat survived."

"Obviously, it would have ended up imprisoned in the pyramid forever!"

"It would've died."

"Because it didn't have anything to eat and drink?"

"Right, and no air or light. Cats hate the dark—did you know that?"

"Yes, but they have infrared eyes to see at night. Lucky things."

"Yes, but the scribe's cat was still scared of being imprisoned, even if it did have infrared eyes, like you say. But as the slaves pushed enormous blocks of stone around the cherry tree and his owner refused to help him come down, the poor cat cried its heart out.

"Everyone pleaded with the scribe to climb up the cherry tree and save the cat before it was too late, but he replied that a cat worthy of a pharaoh knows how to get down a cherry tree."

"That's a bit cruel."

"A bit. But when the slaves, exhausted, were about to place the very last block of stone in position, the cat pulled its claws out of the bark it had been clinging on to and came down the tree in two or three jumps. It was safe."

"Was the pharaoh happy with his special cat?"

"So happy, he gave it the gift of eternal life."

"Oh wow. Does that mean the cat is still around somewhere?"

"Must be."

I sit in silence, but I smile to myself. "That cat certainly wanted to learn to climb down trees!"

"To live in fear, Mafalda, is to not live at all."

I have a massive smile on my face and a prickling in my eyes. To live in fear is to not live at all, to live in fear is to not live at all. . . . I'm not sure I understand the story about the scribe's cat, but it's nice and it makes me tingle, like Filippo's music.

I turn to Estella, who is climbing down the tree.

"Wait! Where are you going?"

"You have to answer this question, Mafalda. What is essential for you?" She jumps and looks up at me from down below.

"Staying here is essential for me."

"Are you sure?"

"Yes. It's the last thing on my list."

"The old one or the new one?"

"What new one?"

"Well, maybe the old one with a new name. Show me."

My fingers explore the inside of my pocket and flick against a crumpled piece of paper, similar to the demerit note I got with Filippo. I pull it out, and I can't see what's written on it, but I know it's the list. Mafalda's list. *Things I care a lot about (that I won't be able to do anymore).*

Estella is speaking clearly; it's not a dream. Estella has always been truthful with me.

"See? All you have to do is give it a new name: *Things I care a lot about.* You're in the cherry tree, Mafalda. You climbed up in the dark, didn't you?"

I sit in silence again, holding the sheet of paper in my hands.

"If the scribe's cat hadn't realized what was essential for him, he would be long gone by now."

I hang on to my branch with both hands, but a voice inside is telling me something.

"I'm in the dark. I'm scared."

"To live in fear is to not live at all, Mafalda. Come on, I showed you how to get down. Put foot here, remember?"

Okay. I do what she says.

"Like this?"

"Yes, like that. Now, jump. . . ."

"Will you catch me?"

Estella doesn't reply.

"Will you catch me?"

I'm hanging from a branch, one foot in a hole in the trunk, one leg dangling in midair. I don't know how high the branch is. The gray around me is getting lighter. I realize it's morning. My arms are sore, and so are my hands and knees from when I fell on the pavement last night. I'd like to let go, but I'm scared. I think about Cosimo, who never came down from the tree his whole life, and I feel a bit sad. I only lasted one night, or half a night.

"Estella, help me!"

Estella doesn't reply, but I hear her voice in my ears telling me I have to do it on my own. I can't be any worse than a chubby cat, right?

I shut my eyes. The darkness is black, there's no

moon, no North Star. I'm tired. It would be easier to simply let go and fall headfirst. I'd end up in the hospital and they might put me in the same room as Estella. But the thought of that frightens me even more. Estella—and Filippo—are my essential things. I can't give up.

"Never ever give up," I chant. "Never ever give up!"

I open my eyes, take my foot out of the hole in the trunk, and dangle in the dark. The cherry tree seems to move under my fingers, as if giving itself a shake. I slide. I let go. I jump.

24

Things I Care a Lot About

The fall seems to go on forever.

The air is cool and dark on my cheeks.

It's not bad, falling. I feel a lurch in my tummy and in my heart, like the time I went on a roller coaster, which is fun but scary, too. I remember the photo of me, Mom, Dad, and Grandma on a kids' roller coaster. Grandma's hair and my hair were standing on end, our arms were up, mouths wide open, teeth flashing (hers ultra-white and false). Grandma loved throwing her arms in the air on rides. I remember her screaming, not in fear, and I remember the camera flash. The bright, white light.

As I fall, I see myself in a flash, like another Mafalda falling in front of me, only she doesn't have the dark in her eyes. We fall together, and she tells me my pigtails are standing up on end, my arms that were holding the branch are still raised, my clothes puffed full of air. I look funny. "Open your eyes," she says. "It's fun!"

I open my eyes, and there's light everywhere. The monsters are cartoon characters, and they're stamping their feet along with Grandma, Ravina, Estella, Filippo, and Ottimo Turcaret. Cosimo and Viola are there. They clap at my fall; they're clear and distinct, together they're like circus performers, and the girl falling in front of me is laughing and pointing her finger up, so before I land, I too look up to the sky, and I count all the stars in the universe.

I'm only a centimeter away. I can feel it. The girl falling with me waves goodbye and whizzes off up to the sky, holding on to a string of red balloons she found who knows where, flying over the top of the tree, higher than the school roof. By now she's playing soccer in the night, a star for a ball. Grandma is in the goal, between the moon and the North Star.

My sneakers touch the concrete on the playground sooner than I thought, and my ankles fall on top of them, knees right after, then my bottom, my back, my shoulders, and my hair. I find myself with my hands on the ground, curled up like an empty bag, with sore feet, but all in one piece.

The dark is still dark. I get up inside it and am about to shout out a name, but I can't remember it; I can only remember my own.

"Mafalda!"

Dad's voice comes running toward me from far away. It's a voice full of fast breathing and maybe even tears, although I'll only know for sure when I smell it.

Dad opens the school gate, banging it, the metal screeching, then runs, throws himself to his knees when he reaches me, and squeezes me as tight, as tight as anything. "Promise me you'll never run away again. Promise," he says, his nose deep in my hair.

"Okay."

He moves a little, and I feel his face in front of mine. His tears smell of chamomile and log fire. Nice. He has his arms round my shoulders. Estella used to do this too.

"How did you find me?"

"Are you all right? Are you all in one piece? I saw you falling from the tree."

"I didn't fall. I was climbing down. How did you find me?"

"We followed your tracks. The neighbors saw you going out the back."

"The not-nice ones?"

"Yes. They're not that bad. They're just shy. They helped us find you."

"Then?"

"I'll tell you everything at home. It's cold. Do you know what time it is?" He stops and I know he's smiling; I hear it in his voice. "It's Grandma's *absolute* favorite time of day."

Something weird happens when I realize what he's getting at. A sun seems to pop out behind my eyes, spreading heat across my face. "Dawn, just like her name?"

He pats my head. "Yes, Mafalda, that was her name. Let's go home."

"Shall we count how many steps there are between the cherry tree and its smell?"

Mom jingles the keys to the new house, and Ottimo Turcaret slips through the door a second before she pulls it shut.

"Mom, it wouldn't be fair. I can smell the cherry tree's perfume as soon as I open my bedroom window!" We cross the street lined with Mary's eyes flowers and we're behind the school, where the organic vegetable garden is. I hear Ottimo Turcaret's padded landing as he sneaks in to do his business—it makes me laugh.

"You're right; it's not fair. I'll take you inside."

A rush of warm air caresses my cheek, then I hear the secret whistle that's not all that secret. I turn to Mom.

"I get it. You want to go alone. All right, I'll be here when you come out."

She kisses me, then starts to walk away. I know she's secretly watching me and thinks I don't know. I put a foot on the first step. Fast steps come running down toward me from the top. It's like I can almost see the person in front of me—straight back, legs wide, hands on hips. Filippo.

"Grab on to me; let's go in."

We go up the stairs, and he tells me I'm as slow as a boring slow song. This makes me think of our band, which is just a duo for now. "Are we practicing today?"

"Yes, at three o'clock."

"What are we singing? 'Yellow Submarine'?"

"No, a new song."

"Okay. I'll put it on the list."

"What list?"

"A new one. *Things I care a lot about.*"

"Do you have it with you?"

"Yes."

"Let's see."

I pull a sheet of paper, folded in four, from my pocket and hand it to Filippo.

"Whoa, look at your writing! I can't read a word."

His voice is like butterscotch. He manages to struggle through my new list.

> *Things I Care a Lot About*
> *Music*
> *Ottimo Turcaret*
> *Stories*
> *Skiing and sledding with Dad or Filippo*
> *Racing on a bike behind Filippo*
> *Guessing the time by the sun on my face*
> *Having a best friend*
> *Flowers and their smell*
> *Traveling to a different place every year*
> *Climbing up cherry trees*
> *Climbing down cherry trees*
> *Not being alone*
> *Loving someone*
> *Being strong like an Amazon*
> *Writing at least one book*

He stops. "It's great. I'll write it out neater for you at lunch."

I feel happy. I'm so happy, I even forget to turn

round and wave to Mum, who's still standing at the school gate. She's happy too because she knows that my essential was finding at least one true friend, and when your eleven-year-old daughter finds a true friend in the dark, well, I think you'd have no choice but to be happy.

"Will you help me write the book?"

Filippo slips the list back into my pocket and takes my hand. The bell rings; it's time to go in.

"Okay. Do you know how it's going to start?"

I smile. "Yes. It starts like this. . . . *All children are scared of the dark. . . .*"

Epilogue

Dear Mafalda,

A while ago I told you that a not-nice friend of mine took away a bit of me, do you remember? Well, Estella does not tell lies. Only truth. So, I think you should know that it wasn't a friend, but a very nasty illness, and the illness has come back, and now it's trying to take away another bit of me, maybe even all of me. That's why I'm in the hospital and couldn't do our secret whistle.

I'm absolutely certain that when you

read this letter, I'll already be living with your grandma and your giant in the tree trunk, and we'll be having a whale of a time together. You can come and see us whenever you want—just climb up the tree and put your feet where I told you the first time we met a few years ago. We also talked about our lists that day, and I showed you mine. As time went by, I thought about it and started a new one for the things that were essential to me but that I could still do even with only one breast. You gave me the idea, Mafalda, when you started your list of things that you don't need eyes to do, which I think is much more difficult. I hope you found many things to put on your list because you are a true Amazon, a little princess in the trees, and the secret daughter of Sherlock Holmes. I only have one thing on my list—to find a true friend. It's also my essential thing.

I'll see you in the cherry tree, Mafalda. Meanwhile, have lots and lots of fun. Live every day like it's your eleventh birthday.

Yours, Estella from Transylvania, Queen of the Amazons